Prais
Veteran.
D0851828

Liz Andre... ...ough the Fire

"This story is full of all the emotional turmoil, attitude, and sexual tension I've come to really enjoy from Ms. Andrews's storylines. There's nothing quite like a spunky girl who's not afraid to tell you how it is to bring a man out of his self-absorption."

—Chrissy Dionne, *Romance Junkies*

"As always, Andrews comes through with the perfect amount of turmoil to leave you wanting more."

—*Literary Nymphs Reviews*

Rachel Bo's *Risen from Ash*

"Ms. Bo has a delightful BDSM story wrapped up with love. Overall this was a wonderful BDSM romance and I highly suggest it to those who love the genre."

—Julie Esparza, *Just Erotic Romance Reviews*

"With realistic characters, sexual encounters that heat up the screen, and a premise that is completely believable, *Veterans: Risen from Ash* is a story you won't want to miss."

—Trang Black, *eCataRomance Reviews*

ISBN 1-59632-673-5
ISBN 13: 978-1-59632-673-6
VETERANS 1: THROUGH THE FIRE
Copyright © May 2008 by Loose Id, LLC
Cover Art by Croco Designs
Cover Design by April Martinez

Publisher acknowledges the authors and copyright holders of the individual works, as follows:
THROUGH THE FIRE
Copyright © November 2007 by Liz Andrews
RISEN FROM ASH
Copyright © November 2007 by Rachel Bo

DISCLAIMER: Many of the acts described in our BDSM/fetish titles can be dangerous. Please do not try any new sexual practice, whether it be fire, rope, or whip play, without the guidance of an experienced practitioner. Neither Loose Id nor its authors will be responsible for any loss, harm, injury or death resulting from use of the information contained in any of its titles.

This book is an original publication of Loose Id®. Each individual story herein was previously published in e-book format only by Loose Id® and is a work of fiction. Any similarity to actual persons, events or existing locations is entirely coincidental.

Printed in the U.S.A. by
Lightning Source, Inc.
1246 Heil Quaker Blvd
La Vergne TN 37086

Contents

THROUGH THE FIRE

Liz Andrews

Dedication

To Christy and Allie, for inviting me to be a part of this Veterans series and to Rachel, Mechele, and Bobby, for their wonderful contributions.

To Lena, you are my rock; thank you for all your support and encouragement, especially when I act like a crazy woman.

And to all the veterans and soldiers currently serving their country, if you are far away from your loved ones, may you be home soon.

Chapter One

Kena Rutherford would have never in a million years figured she'd get caught skinny-dipping in a client's pool. Of course with her bad luck, she really should have. Peeking over the edge of the pool, she could see a figure moving around the kitchen. Well, technically, the kitchen of the client's son. She could only pray whoever it was would stay indoors long enough for her to sneak out of the pool and get dressed.

See, this is what I get for breaking the rules. The worst part was, as the owner of TLC, her home-based cleaning service, she was breaking her own rules. *Damn dummy.*

As she tried to hide in the shadows, she cursed her lack of judgment and the scorching summer heat. After spending all day cleaning the two-story house from top to bottom she'd needed something to ease her pain. Thanks to the pool guy she subcontracted to clean it, the pool was crisp and clean and had beckoned to her as she gathered her things to leave for the day. The sun had set and the idea of swimming nude was a decadent fantasy that just wouldn't leave her alone.

No one will ever know, she had told herself. Just a little dip. Who could it hurt? The answer apparently was her, and her house-cleaning business. Her reputation was at stake here. Something she probably should have thought of before she jumped buck naked into the water.

Now she was mentally kicking herself for her stupidity. She cringed when she realized it was about to get worse. Much, much worse. The snick of the French doors opening was the only warning she had before the man who had been inside the house walked out onto the patio.

"I was able to take an earlier plane, Mother. I just didn't see a reason to…well I'm calling you now, aren't I?"

Damn it, he was the owner. She should just kiss her ass good-bye. If he was anything like his mother, she was so fired. When Mrs. Garrett had called about contracting with TLC, she had gone on and on about how her precious son could only have the best of the best. Her high-handed tone had gotten on Kena's nerves immediately and if she didn't need the contract, she might have turned the overbearing woman down flat.

Unfortunately, since she was just getting her business off the ground, she couldn't afford to pass up paying customers. Moreover, in this case she didn't think she'd have too much personal contact with the client or the owner. Mrs. Garrett didn't live in the home and her son was *supposed* to be out of town.

Kena pressed herself against the edge of the pool, keeping her head down to avoid being seen. "Fuck. Fuck. Fuck," she muttered softly to herself.

The sound of a patio chair being pulled out made her heart sink. Apparently he was making himself at home…in his own home. The bastard. What the hell was she going to do now?

There were a few bursts of input from him, but he was mostly listening. In her mind's eye she could see where she had tossed her clothing, just shy of the bottom step. As long as he stayed on the patio and didn't venture farther out she would be safe. Unfortunately for her, as soon as the thought flitted across her brain, she heard him sigh.

"Look, Mother, let me call you back. I'm tired and I need to shower. Yes. I know. Give my love to Dad."

The sound of the phone being clicked off was deafening as was the echo of his feet walking across the wooden decking.

"You might as well come on out. I know you're in there."

Kena froze in terror as she listened to his words.

Damn, damn, damn.

"Look, I don't want to call the cops, but if you don't get out of the pool, I'll have to do something. You're trespassing."

"No, please don't do that."

"Give me one good reason not to."

"I'm your housekeeper. My name's Kena Rutherford."

"Sorry, try again. I don't have a housekeeper." She peeked her head up just in time to see him pick up the phone.

"Please don't call the police. I'm sorry, but I can't get out of the pool." Kena was terrified. It was going to be bad enough explaining to him about using the pool and skinny-dipping, but explaining it to the police was definitely something she didn't want to do. Taking a deep breath she forged ahead.

"Your mother hired my company, TLC, to open your house. I guess she wanted it aired out before you got home, but you surprised me, I mean her, when you arrived early."

"It still doesn't explain why you're in my pool, and why can't you get out?" She jumped when she heard his voice directly overhead and realized he had moved from the patio and was now standing right next to the pool. Thankfully the lights were limited to the area surrounding the house and didn't shine down directly into the pool, but she still felt vulnerable because of her nakedness.

"Ahh, well, I don't have on a swimsuit." Looking up at him she immediately felt intimidated, no thanks to the way he was standing with his arms crossed as he stared down at her, his profile in shadow.

Without uttering a word, he turned and walked back toward the patio, and opened an outside storage shed filled with towels. Kena used the opportunity to size him up. He was muscular without being fat, with broad shoulders that stretched the confines of the blue T-shirt he was wearing. His reddish-brown hair was trimmed close to his head, reminding her that Mrs. Garrett had mentioned her son was coming home from Iraq.

Before she knew it, he was back at the edge of the pool. "Okay, here's a towel. Now you can get out."

"If you'll just lay it there and turn around…" Her voice trailed off at the shaking of his head.

"No way. I'm not going to take the chance you'll run the moment my back is turned."

Kena gasped at his audacity. How dare he accuse her of such a reprehensible act? Of course, the only knowledge he had of her was she was a trespasser and sometime nudist; consequently, it wasn't likely he had a very good impression of her character.

"Look, I promise not to run."

"Nope. Out, now." He held out the towel and turned his head slightly, in an almost imperceptible nod to her modesty.

Kena stewed for a moment, but eventually scrambled out of the pool. Irritated, she stomped over to him and snatched the towel from his hand. "There was no need to be rude."

"Rude?"

"Yes, rude. A gentleman would have turned his back. I hope you got your jollies." She wrapped the thick terry cloth around her body, her irritation overriding any embarrassment she may have felt. If she let the anger go, she might have to analyze just what a colossal mess she was in.

"Words can't explain my excitement," he commented dryly.

Kena knew she'd better start talking quick. Her livelihood was at stake here and the next few minutes might be the difference between her having a business tomorrow or hitting the unemployment line.

"You're really not catching me at my best."

"You don't say." The sardonic smirk didn't alleviate her nervousness.

"I'm usually very professional. I mean your mother only wanted to hire the best and she came to TLC. What does that tell you?"

"She's still a cheapskate. I hate to break it to you, sister, but my mother pretends to be all hoity-toity, but she'll squeeze a penny as far as she can. If she hired your company, it was because she could get the most out of you for the least amount of money."

"*Sister* -- is that some veiled reference to my race?"

"Give me a break. You should be more concerned about the fact my mother pulled one over on you."

When Kena had been negotiating with Mrs. Garrett, she thought she might have given in a bit too soon. Now her son was confirming her worst fears; her lack of a business degree might be working against her. Nevertheless, she wasn't going to let him see her sweat.

"Not really. I have a good business and I perform honest work for a good wage. If your mother thought she was getting a good deal, she was right. Being economical will help my business grow. She'll probably tell her friends and before you know it my business will thrive."

"You're living in a dream world. She'd never tell her friends because then they'd find out what a skinflint she is. If you were expecting to get references from her, I wouldn't hold my breath."

She could almost feel herself deflating at his words. She *had* expected to make a lot of contacts through her. Unfortunately, it seemed swimming nude in the pool hadn't been the first nail in her coffin but the last. She was going to be right back where she started, battling with the big name companies for a piece of the pie.

The cleaning business was a fickle one. People didn't mind paying for services when times were good. But when money got tight those extra special things were the first to go.

Kena wrapped her arms around herself, suddenly feeling the chill and wondered if it was due to the night air or reality slapping her in the face.

Baldwin knew he was being an ass, but he really couldn't care less. He was tired from the flight in and his leg was aching. It was ridiculous that his leg injury was the one thing bothering him the most in this day straight from hell, but there was nothing logical about how his mind worked. The best thing about this day had actually been finding the bathing beauty in his pool.

He had spent the last three hours traveling and was in no mood for company. Even the sexy, naked kind.

And she was very sexy, with smooth chocolaty brown skin and dark, flashing eyes. Her dark, wet hair was curly from her swim and coiled around her ears in a pixie kind of way. Taller than average for a woman, she had legs that didn't stop. She wasn't too thin, but had very nice curves and if the situation had been different, he wouldn't have minded seeing more of them.

"So, Kena was it? Do you want to explain why I came home to find you naked in my pool?"

"Would it have been better if you found me naked in your garage?" She'd obviously regained her early bravado.

"Excuse me?" He cocked a brow. "Would you like me to cut the question segment short and go straight to calling the police?"

"Calling the police for skinny-dipping? Come on."

"You're trespassing."

"Not really. I'm supposed to be here. I told you, your parents hired me to open up the house for you."

"I sincerely doubt they hired a nude cleaning service." His mother was one of the most uptight women he knew. He couldn't imagine for a second she'd do something daring ...and, well, fun.

"I don't clean in the nude." She had the audacity to sound offended. How amusing.

"Says the chick in the bath towel."

"Okay, look, I know this doesn't look good."

"I wouldn't go that far," he drawled.

"I'm sorry. My behavior was completely uncalled for. I abused my authority and I have no excuses. I will only say I thought no one would be home and I never meant to harm anyone. It's been a really long day and the pool just looked terribly inviting. It was like it was calling to me."

She was very sincere in her argument and probably didn't realize she had been leaning forward as she spoke, causing the towel she was holding together to gape slightly. He was getting tempting peeks of her breasts every few seconds, and like most men would, he felt his mood improving considerably. Bad day or not, boobs were always nice to look at.

"Calling to you, huh? What was it saying?"

She blinked her eyes, as if shocked by his joking tone. "Kena, come swim in me. I'm lonely."

"Lonely, I see. It's a good thing I'm home then. I plan to use the pool a lot." Frankly he could probably use the pool right now. He had been wondering how much longer he could stand there talking to her. The throbbing ache in his leg told him that he had just about reached his limit. Turning back toward the patio he tried to figure out if he could make it back to the chair before he fell flat on his face.

"Is everything okay?"

"I just need to sit down."

"Let me help you."

Despite the shooting pain radiating down his leg, Baldwin still stiffened up at her words. "I don't need help. I'm not an invalid."

"But you're hurt."

"It's nothing," he lied.

"Don't be stupid. You look like I should be yelling out 'timber' any moment now."

"Very funny, but you couldn't be farther from the truth." He tried to take a step forward and could feel his leg beginning to buckle. *I will not fall.* Maybe if he repeated it enough times he'd actually believe it himself. Unfortunately, it wasn't meant to be and he could sense himself start to shift.

Just at that moment, Kena rushed to his side and wrapped her arm around his waist, helping to support him. He slowly made his way to the chairs on the patio. Collapsing in the lounger, Baldwin closed his eyes to the pain shooting through his body. He could hear her heading into the house and wondered for a moment if she was getting away while the getting was good.

He wouldn't blame her. It wasn't as if he was in any shape to chase her down. But surprisingly, he heard her returning to the patio just a few moments later.

"Which one?"

"Which one what?" Opening his eyes, he saw three bottles of pills being waved wildly in front of him.

"Which one is for pain?"

"Where did you get those?" He thought he'd buried them in his bag along with every other piece of painful memorabilia from his time in the hospital.

"The crack dealer outside. What do you think?" Kena shook her head in obvious disgust. "I rummaged through your luggage."

"I don't want them." He needed them, but he didn't want them. Pills were an addiction he didn't want to start. No way was he getting hooked like some junkie in a back alley somewhere. He planned to heal from his injury the old-fashioned way, through force of will and hard work.

"But you'll take it anyway."

"I will, will I?"

"Yes, because if you won't take them from me, I'll call your mother and I'm sure she'll be more than happy to come over."

Snatching the bottles from her hand, he glared mena-cingly at her, but she didn't budge. As he sorted through the medicine to find the one for pain, he cursed her interfering busybody soul. Who the hell did she think she was, telling him what to do? And threatening him with his mother? That was a low-down, dirty trick.

After locating the right bottle, he tried to open it on his own, but couldn't even summon the strength for such a simple task. Kena finally pried the bottles from his hand and opened the one he'd been struggling with with a simple twist of her wrist.

Show off.

Baldwin laid his head back and closed his eyes, drifting off for a brief moment. Unfortunately, instead of hearing the smooth mellow sounds of his jazz alarm waking him up, it was Kena clearing her throat that roused him.

He opened his eyes and focused on the glass of water she held out to him. Taking the water and pills from her, he swallowed them quickly, praying they would kick in fast. "Thanks."

"You're welcome. I figured I was already in trouble for the skinny-dipping; therefore, it wouldn't matter much to go one step further and search your luggage."

"Not close."

"Huh?"

"If you think digging up pain pills negates me finding you trespassing naked in the pool, it's not even close."

"Actually, no, I was thinking I was being helpful because it was the humane thing to do. I guess I didn't realize you were really the devil incarnate. Excuse the hell out of me."

"Nobody does something without expecting something out of it." He resented the hell out of the fact someone had to take care of him. It went against everything he was. He was used to being the one who took care of things. The bitterness he felt ate away at him. He hated feeling weak and helpless.

"Actually, yes, they do. But you wouldn't know anything about those types of people." Kena had started to back away as she spoke, heading toward her clothes which were piled at the edge of the patio.

"Where do you think you're going?"

"Home, if that's permissible."

He could hear her struggling to quickly get dressed and suppressed the urge he had to turn around and peek. "Right, home." She might not say she thought they were even, but she was no longer trying to talk her way out of the trespassing.

"Um, I hate to say this, but I don't even know your name."

He cocked open an eye and noted she now stood before him dressed. Although not quite as good as totally nude, she was still easy on the eyes. He tried to focus on her question. She wanted to know his name. "Baldwin Garrett."

Leaning forward, she shook the hand he offered. "Hello, Mr. Garrett."

"No Mr. It was Captain, but now it's just plain Baldwin."

"Sorry, but Baldwin isn't plain. It's kind of..."

"Ostentatious?"

"I wasn't going to say it, but it's certainly not Joe or Bob."

"It's a family name. When my grandfather realized he wasn't going to have any boys, he made my mother promise to name her firstborn Baldwin in order for the family name to live on."

"You were the lucky firstborn, huh?"

"First and only. But I wouldn't say lucky."

"Okay, well, I'll see you later." Kena started to leave, but then turned back around. "Um, you do know I'm coming back, right?"

"No, I didn't even know you existed until twenty minutes ago."

"That's what I was worried about," she muttered under her breath. "Here's the deal. Not only did your mom hire me to open the house, but she hired me to come in three times a week to clean."

"Great." He couldn't wait to confront his mother with this newest piece of evidence of her once again interfering in his life.

"I guess I'll be seeing you then."

Baldwin nodded in lieu of speaking. There was no point in protesting, God had stopped listening to him a long time ago.

Chapter Two

When Kena arrived at Baldwin's house two days later, she wondered what reception she might get. Especially after she leaned on the doorbell for ten minutes straight and there was no answer. After a few moments of indecision, she pulled out the key she'd been given by Mrs. Garrett and unlocked the front door.

"Hello, anyone home?" Her call echoed throughout the house, but there was no response. Maybe he wasn't home.

Heading into the kitchen, she set down her cleaning supplies and looked around the room. It looked like a tornado had hit the place. When she'd left there the other night, the room had been spotless, but now dirty dishes were piled in the sink and remnants from past meals littered the countertop. How one man could make such a mess in two days was beyond her.

As she passed the French doors, a blur from the backyard caught her eye. Opening the door she heard voices in the backyard and realized Baldwin was in the pool with someone, a woman from the sounds of it.

"Oh Baldwin, you are doing such a great job. I can't believe it. I'm so proud of you."

Kena almost puked at the high-pitched, little girl voice coming from the bleach blonde bimbo sitting on the edge of the pool. She doubted the man could even hear the inane encouragement since he was swimming laps, not even lifting his head as he hit the edge of the pool but performing a flip turn to continue his strokes.

BBB was now clapping her hands wildly and cheering. Kena shook her head with disgust. Although she had barely met the man the other night, for some reason she had thought he had a brain in his head. But with a ding-a-ling girlfriend like that, she figured she must have seriously overestimated his intelligence.

Quietly closing the French doors, she popped her earbuds in and, singing to herself softly, began to work her way through the house. She always left the kitchen as the last room to clean for two reasons. One, people tended to leave dishes in other rooms. And after numerous instances of thinking she was done in the kitchen only to find one more dirty glass, she had changed her routine to always do a thorough walk-through of the house first. Second, she liked to finish in the kitchen by mopping the floor. She could then leave from the back door knowing every room was in tip-top shape.

When she reached Baldwin's bedroom, she had to grin. Right again. There were a stack of dirty dishes by the bed. Single men all tended to be the same and left their houses pretty much intact for her to clean. Women and families, on the other hand, tried to clean up before she arrived. She wasn't really sure why, since they were paying her to clean, but if it made them happy and her job less taxing, who was she to complain.

As she made up his bed she couldn't help but fantasize about what he might look like naked lying there in front of her. Ever since she had talked to him the other night she had begun to have stray thoughts of him in the most inappropriate way. Not as a professional would have about their client's son, but as a woman would a man. It really was a shame he was surly, because she could definitely go for him.

After finishing cleaning upstairs, she returned the dirty dishes to the kitchen before starting the laundry. Although she had thought Mrs. Garrett was crazy to want to hire her to come in three days a week for a single man who lived alone, she was beginning to reassess her doubts. Baldwin was a first-class slob, dropping his clothes where he took them off. The only good thing she could say was she saw no evidence of the BBB staying there. It was ridiculous, since she should have cared less, but there it was.

When she finally returned to the kitchen, Kena pulled up short to find Baldwin in the kitchen, dripping from the pool. He stood in front of the sink, head titled back as he drained a glass of water. She watched as his throat worked to swallow the liquid. His body was lean and muscled. A work of art, except for one thing marring his perfection.

She gasped as she caught sight of the scars covering his left leg. It looked like it had been through a meat grinder, the flesh red and puckered from the injuries done to him.

Unfortunately her response caused a chain reaction. Baldwin turned at the noise and his leg began to collapse.

She watched, as if in slow motion, the glass fall from his hand as he tried to catch himself from falling. As the glass hit the sink it shattered, sending shards flying through the air.

"Oh shit." She rushed forward to help, but Baldwin pushed her away, as he gripped the sink to stop his fall. When he was finally upright once more, he slowly turned to her.

"What the hell are you doing here?"

"I told you I'd be back to clean the house."

"Is this going to become a habit?"

"What?"

"Me coming home to find you sneaking around in some part of my house, only to have you save me from falling on my ass."

"I wasn't exactly sneaking. I rang the bell first. After you didn't answer I let myself in with the key your mother gave me. I'm working."

"Really? It seems like you're standing around gawking. Like what you see?" Baldwin's mocking face dared her to say no, but she could glimpse a bit of vulnerability there as well.

She knew he was referring to his injured leg and she had to admit she'd been shocked at first. Sure the scars weren't attractive and she'd never try to convince him otherwise. But more alarming to her was what those scars represented -- the horror of the injury he must have suffered and the pain he constantly endured. But she instinctively knew he wouldn't want what he would consider pity; therefore, she decided to deliberately misunderstand his question. What's more, it wasn't completely untruthful.

"I like what I see; I like it a lot." Kena infused her voice with the attraction she felt toward him. And her words were no lie. He was a handsome man and she'd have to be dead not to notice his washboard abs and chiseled muscles, especially with him standing there in nothing more than swimming trunks.

His brow furrowed as if he were trying to decide if she was serious or not. "You get off on seeing deformed cripples?"

"You're hardly deformed."

"Yeah, right. That's why you freaked when you saw me."

"Excuse me, but I wasn't the one freaking." She shook her head. "Look, this conversation is getting us nowhere. Why don't you just stay still and let me clean up the glass."

"No, I can clean it up."

"Don't be ridiculous. You have no shoes on. Your feet will get cut to ribbons. Let me do my job. I'm a pro at cleaning."

Before he could argue further, she grabbed the broom and dustpan and went to work sweeping up the broken glass. At one point she was on her knees before him and happened to glance up. The outline of his cock in his swimming trunks was more than obvious. However, it was the smoldering look in his eyes that truly caught her off guard and caused her to stumble as she tried to stand.

"Watch out. We don't need both of us falling over."

Flustered at knowing he realized her discomfort, she grasped at a change in subject as she quickly made her way to her feet and dumped the swept up glass.

"What happened to your little friend?"

"Who…oh, you mean Gloria? She had to go home."

"Oh, too bad."

"How did you know she was here?" Baldwin made his way to the table and sat heavily in one of the chairs. Kena wanted to recommend he find his pain medication, but after everything that had occurred up to this point she didn't know if he would appreciate her suggestions.

"I noticed you both outside when I arrived."

"And you didn't let me know you were here?"

"You were busy swimming laps and she was busy being your cheerleader."

"Cheerleader?"

"Go, Baldwin, you can do it, I know you can. Ooo, I'm so proud of you." Kena mimicked in Gloria's little girl voice.

Baldwin laughed aloud at her impression. "She's really a friend of the family. My mother sent her over to give me encouragement during my physical therapy."

"She seems to be doing an excellent job."

"Just like everyone else, she's doing what she has to do to get what she wants."

Ouch! "I'm not trying to defend the woman, but do you know you have a very low opinion of people?"

"Please, everyone's a liar. Some are just better at it than others."

"Including you?"

"Especially me."

Intrigued at his honesty, Kena pressed on. "Who do you lie to?"

"Myself."

Baldwin's nightmares from last night must have put him in an introspective mood this morning because he doubted he would have revealed anything as personal otherwise. Being back home was an everyday reminder of the guilt he constantly carried with him.

"Just wondered why you thought you needed to lie to yourself. Can't you at least be honest with yourself?"

"You wouldn't understand."

"I guess the maid is too stupid to understand." Kena pursed her lips and cocked her head.

"That's not what I said. Don't put words into my mouth."

"Then why don't you explain it to me."

"How much time do you have?"

"Oh please, it can't be as bad as you think."

"You don't think so, do you?"

"You're alive. You made it back from the war in one piece."

Baldwin pointed to his injured leg. From her earlier gasp he knew for a fact she hadn't missed the less-than-perfect limb he now had. "I wouldn't exactly call this one piece."

"It's still attached to your body. You're still able to use it."

"Barely."

"Wasn't that you doing an impression of Matt Biondi out there in the pool a few minutes ago?"

"You talk a lot shit for someone whose body is in perfect working order." He ran his hand through his hair with frustration.

"And you whine an awful lot for someone who is pretty blessed."

"You call this blessed?"

"As matter of fact I do."

"Then you're more naïve than I realized."

"What's horrible about your life? You're rich, you're white, and you live in America, which in my book means you have the world at your feet."

"I'm not rich, my family is."

"Does your argument even make sense to you? I'm not rich, my family is. Come on."

"Yes, as a matter of fact it does."

Kena glanced around the kitchen and then back at him with a look of disbelief. "Have you seen where you live, Mr. I'm Not Rich? I had to be frisked just to drive on the street."

"I inherited this house from my grandfather. I'm a simple captain in the air force, end of story."

Baldwin was starting to get angry. He wasn't sure, but somehow Kena had found a way to push all his buttons and was poking at those lies he often told to himself.

"I think it's just the beginning."

"I think it's time we call it day. Why don't you pack up your stuff and head home."

"And to think I was just beginning to believe we were making some headway with your 'woe is me' problem."

"My only problem is a self-righteous maid with a God complex. Why don't you climb back on the broom you used to sweep up my kitchen and fly away."

"And leave all this lovely splendor behind? Sorry, Richie Rich, some of us have to work for a living. It's my job to clean your house."

"I don't exactly need anyone to pick up after me. This was all my mother's idea."

"Really? Have you seen this place? As far as I can tell your mother is doing you a favor by hiring me. You're a grade A slob. No one could possibly want to live like this and for the life of me, I can't figure out why you do."

"Did you ever think I can't do some of those things because of my injuries?"

"Oh, stop feeling sorry for yourself."

"I don't take orders from little girls."

"In case you haven't noticed I'm neither little nor a girl. I'm a grown ass woman who has opinions and has the freedom to express them. If you don't like it, too bad."

Baldwin didn't like hearing her say all the things he hadn't even admitted to himself. Arguing with her was like arguing with a pit bull. He just wanted to shut her up and could only think of one good way to accomplish his goal.

Standing up, he moved over to where she was standing against the counter. Baldwin watched her eyes widen as he herded her into the corner.

"You think you're so smart and you have all the answers, but you don't. Don't bother to tell me your opinions, because I didn't ask for them."

She opened her mouth as if to speak, but he didn't allow her the opportunity. Slipping his hand around the nape of her neck, he tilted her head back and bent to capture her lips in a bruising kiss. It wasn't a kiss of love or even affection, but one filled with pent-up desire and frustration.

Her lips, at first cold and unyielding, parted for his kiss. At her surrender, he slipped his tongue inside her mouth to explore more of her sweet taste. He pressed his body against hers, groaning as his straining erection aligned with her softness. She wasn't totally unaffected either. Her nipples were hard little points pressing into his chest.

Breaking their kiss, he buried his head in her neck, inhaling her unique scent. Baldwin pulled her shirt up, exposing inches of her soft brown skin to his touch, and cupped her breast through the lacy material of her bra. She gasped at the contact, her hands gripping his arms, but not hindering his movement.

Grasping her nipple firmly, he rolled it between his fingers, changing her gasp from one of surprise to one of yearning. While one hand remained on her breast, the other moved from her neck to her waistband, trying unsuccessfully to unbutton her jeans.

Suddenly, Baldwin felt her hands pushing at his shoulders. "I'm sorry, but I can't. Not like this."

It took him a minute to hear what she was saying, but when he did, he took a deep breath before stepping away from her. "You better leave while you can."

Kena looked as if she wanted to say something, but finally slipped around him and picked up her purse as she headed out the door.

Damn it all to hell. Baldwin felt the need to pick something up and break it, but since he'd already broken one glass this morning, he curbed his impulses. His mind was warring with his body. He knew she was probably right and they needed to stop. But reason wasn't part of the equation when he found himself hard and wanting.

Yet it wasn't just an itch he needed to scratch, because if that was the case, Baldwin had plenty of opportunity. Gloria had done her damnedest to convince him all he needed was a little loving from her to feel right as rain. He'd even tried kissing her, but there was no desire there; in fact, he'd felt nothing at all.

But with Kena it was a different story. She drove him crazy with her questions and her opinions and most of all her body. He'd been fantasizing for the last two days of the curves he'd only caught faint glimpses of the other night. Unfortunately, thoughts like that got him nowhere, especially since he'd ordered her to leave.

His attention was diverted from Kena by the phone ringing. "Hello."

"Baldwin, I was just calling to see how things were going."

Hearing his father's blustering voice expressing such concern for his well-being was a strange event. Although he'd always felt closer to his father than to his mother, neither parent was the overly affectionate sort.

"Everything's going fine, Dad."

"I only wondered because Gloria stopped by."

Just as he'd thought. Gloria was a spy for his parents. He shouldn't be cynical, but it was hard not to with the evidence staring him in the face.

"And what did she have to say that would cause you to pick up the phone?"

"Now don't start blaming Gloria. We're all just worried about you. You're pushing yourself too hard."

This was the same argument he'd heard from the doctors when he began refusing the pain medications and pushed his rehabilitation past acceptable standards. They wanted him to see a therapist, but Baldwin refused. He knew why he was pushing himself so hard, but he didn't feel the need to share it with someone who might be likely to have him committed.

"Don't worry, Dad. I'm doing fine."

"I happened to overhear Gloria sharing with your mother some private girl talk. There isn't something else we need to know, is there?"

He wondered if this was his dad's euphemistic way of asking if he was impotent. Both his parents would flip a lid if he told them he wasn't interested in Gloria, but in the hot owner of the cleaning service they'd hired for him. She wasn't exactly of the same social standing, something his parents held in high regard. Thankfully, he wouldn't have to have that conversation since he didn't plan to share the details of his sex life with his father.

"No, Dad, there's nothing else you need to know. Thanks for the call, but everything is fine."

Baldwin hung up the phone and looked around the room, which was still in chaos, much like his life. He just hoped he hadn't scared her away completely. Kena made him feel and instead of running from those feelings he wanted to explore them; he hadn't *wanted* to do much of anything for a very long time now.

Chapter Three

Kena rummaged through her supplies as she knelt on the rug, but finally threw her hands up in despair. "It's not here. Damn the man, I know I left it there."

Her aunt Donna didn't look up from the book she was reading but asked loudly, "What are you looking for?"

Instead of answering, she continued to mutter to herself. "Stupid asshole made me leave everything there and now I can't do my job."

"For him to be such a stupid asshole, you sure do talk about him an awful lot. It's not as if you don't have any supplies you can't replace." Her aunt finally glanced up and Kena could see her brown eyes twinkling.

For a sixty-three-year-old woman she was still quite fit. When Kena was younger, sixty-three seemed an age when people were old and ill, but her aunt was nothing like her childhood image of an elderly woman. Donna Boden's coal black hair was shot through with a few gray strands and she wore glasses to read, but otherwise she looked better than most women half her age.

Kena had lived with her aunt since she was sixteen years old and her mother, Donna's sister, had died. Her aunt had never married, but Kena was like her own daughter. They didn't have a big family, but it was a loving one. Even after Kena finished school and started her own business she continued to live with her aunt in their old Victorian home. It was kind of rambling for the two of them, but it was familiar.

"I know that look. You think you know something, but you're wrong. I'm only talking about him because he's trying to ruin my life. I needed that job. And I need my supplies. I just can't replace everything at once."

"Weren't you looking for something in particular?" Her aunt pointed out. "I think it sounds like an excuse to me. If the supplies are so important, just go get them."

If only it were as easy as it sounded. But how could she return to his house as if nothing had happened when it felt as if her life had been turned upside down. Baldwin probably hated her, and as much as she was loath to admit it, he had every right to be mad. First she insulted the man in his own home. Then, when he started to kiss her, she suddenly called a halt to everything with no explanation. She really didn't think he was waiting with baited breath for her return after the disastrous way things had ended yesterday.

"I can't go back there. You don't understand."

"Of course I don't, because you really haven't explained anything. You just came in here blustering about how the asshole threw you out and never really shared the details."

Kena buried her face in her hands. "It's because the details are too embarrassing, okay? And truthfully, he didn't really throw me out."

"Nope, not okay. I want to hear." Her aunt put down her book and took off her glasses, sitting up to get the scoop. It reminded Kena of when she'd dated in high school and college and would come home to her aunt waiting up for her. They would sit around and eat ice cream and dissect all the particulars of the date.

Finally, lifting her head in defeat, Kena gave in. "He kissed me and I pushed him away. Then he told me I better leave while I could."

Her aunt raised her eyebrows at the last comment, but her question was directed to the first. "Why did you push him away? Was he a bad kisser?"

"No, that was the problem. His kisses were intoxicating. I didn't want to stop. But he'd started kissing me in anger and I didn't want him to say later it was a mistake. I decided to stop it first."

Her aunt tapped her finger on her lips lightly. "Why was he kissing you in anger? He's not some freak, is he? Because I know I raised you better than to hang around freaks."

Kena laughed and leaned forward to hug her aunt. "You did. And how the heck would I know if he's a freak? Maybe I like freaks." Sobering for a moment, she thought about his actions. "He just seems to be carrying a lot of guilt, from the war I think, and I started pushing his buttons. He probably just kissed me to stop me from bugging him."

"You do have a way of pushing people's buttons."

"Thanks," Kena drawled.

"No problem. I just tell it like it is."

"Don't I know it."

"I still don't see why you can't go back."

"He probably couldn't wait to see the door hit me where the good Lord split me."

"Somehow I doubt it. He was kissing you after all."

"Men are really difficult to understand." Kena flopped down next to her aunt on the couch and took comfort in the arm she wrapped around her. "They need to come with instruction manuals."

"Girl, I know what you mean. Why do you think I never got married? I am too independent. But don't let my example put you off on finding someone who you can spend the rest of your life with."

"Hey, you're assuming a bit much. We were kissing; that's it. Okay, there was a little over the bra action. But it doesn't put us in the married and four children category, not by a long shot."

"So maybe you don't know yet if you want to spend the rest of your life with him. But are you interested in spending some time with him to figure it out?"

Was she? Surprisingly Kena found the answer was in the affirmative. Which only went to show she didn't know up from down when it came to Captain Baldwin Garrett.

"Yes, I think I am. Which really sucks when I may have already screwed everything up."

"No way, not my baby girl. You've just got to go back over there and apologize."

"Apologize. Why should I be the one to apologize?"

"Let me count the ways." Her aunt held up her finger. "First, you admitted you insulted the man. Then, you walked out without talking to him."

"But he --"

"Don't interrupt me. The final reason, and the only one that really matters, is this: you're attracted to the man. You're going to do what you have to to make sure you've got a chance with him. And if it means going over there and saying you're sorry, you'll do it with a smile. Because a good man isn't one you should give up on quickly."

Kena mulled over her words. It was odd to think she'd only known Baldwin a few days and she was interested to see where things could go. Unfortunately, she had no idea if he felt the same way.

"It probably would never work out. I mean we're from two different worlds."

"Really?"

"Yes."

"What world does he come from? Mars? Pluto?"

"You know what I mean."

"No, I don't."

"Fine, we're both from this world, but we couldn't be any more different if we tried. He's white, rich, and had everything handed to him on a silver platter. I'm black, not rich, and I've had to work hard for everything I've ever had. Furthermore, I've met his mother and a more uptight, conservative woman doesn't exist. She'd probably shit a brick if we started dating."

"Shit a brick. Hell, you should date him just to see it."

Her aunt loved to shake people up, especially those like Baldwin's mother who seemed to think they were open-minded while all the while they talked about those not like themselves behind closed doors. She had been an advocate and rabble-rouser from way back. Their family had been active in the civil rights movement and the entire family would get involved, even down to the youngest child. She'd grown up fighting for freedom and believing everyone's voice had a right to be heard.

"I'm not out to change the world, like some people."

"Then shame on you." Her aunt frowned. "I know for a fact I didn't get hosed down by the police and attacked by crazy dogs just for you to sit on the back of the bus all over again."

"I'm not..." Why did she even try? "Everything isn't about the civil rights movement."

"The hell it isn't, especially if the reason you're not going to talk to this man is because his momma might have issues with your skin color and he comes from money and you don't. It's a protest hymn waiting to get sung."

"Those aren't the only reasons." Of course, she couldn't think of any others off the top of her head, but she wasn't going to admit that aloud. "But even you have to admit family is important."

"Then it's a good thing your family is more open than his seems to be. We accept all kinds. More to the point, there's only one difference that really matters, you know that."

"What difference is that?"

"He's a man and you're a woman. All the other stuff can be worked out."

* * *

Baldwin dove into the pool and let the cool water wash over him. He took out his pent-up frustration, cutting through the clear blue liquid with brusque even strokes. The physical activity meant to relax him was having the opposite effect, however, and his mind raced with thoughts of Kena and how things had ended yesterday.

He was a fucking idiot. He should have never let her leave. If he had the chance to do it all again, he would have taken what she'd offered. His one moment of chivalry had left him aching. Thanks to her, he'd tossed and turned all night, finally having to take matters into his own hands, literally. The lackluster experience had left him physically sated, but only briefly.

Unfortunately his dissatisfaction returned tenfold when he awoke this morning. His attempts to distract himself had been fruitless. Even the crisp water did nothing to ease his throbbing cock. He needed to get laid but appeasing his hunger was no simple matter. The idea of being with anyone other than Kena was as unappealing as Gloria had been yesterday.

The only relief from his frustration had been the constant pain in his leg. He'd purposely left his usual swim until dusk, hoping the exercise would tire him out to the point where he would be too exhausted to do anything but sleep tonight. Regrettably it hadn't yet worked. Deciding to take a break, Baldwin stopped and reached out to grab the bottle of water he'd left at the end of the pool, but came up empty.

"Is this what you're looking for?"

Wiping the water off his face, he looked up to see Kena sitting on a lounger next to the pool with the afore-mentioned water bottle. The sight of the cause of his ongoing frustration was both stimulating as well as disconcerting.

Unlike the last two times he'd seen her, she was wearing makeup. Not a lot, but just enough to accentuate her high cheekbones. Her full lips were shining in the fading sunset, begging to be kissed. She was wearing a pink tank top and patterned skirt that ended at her knees, showcasing her long, lean legs.

Rather than show his pleasure at her presence, he held out his hand, requesting the water. "If you don't mind."

As she walked to the edge of the pool, she pursed her lips in obvious annoyance. Leaning down, she handed him the bottle. "I thought maybe we could talk."

Did she now. He unscrewed the cap and took a long swallow before asking, "About?"

Baldwin knew he was being difficult, but he wanted to see where she was going to take this. Besides, the longer she stood there the more opportunity he had to stare at her legs. The view had him hard and wanting her all over again.

"Are you looking up my skirt?" Kena's accusatory tone had him dragging his glance from her alluring charms to her face, which was marred by a frown. He liked her much better when she was smiling.

"What do you expect, darling? When you present the gift in such an enticing package, you can't expect a man not to look."

She rolled her eyes, but the frown faded to be replaced with a Mona Lisa smile. "It wasn't an invitation."

"It certainly seemed that way to me." He noticed she had stepped back, but otherwise had done nothing to dissuade him other than acting affronted, which he believed was just that, an act.

"Look, I came over here to apologize for my actions yesterday."

Baldwin's brow furrowed in displeasure. *Great.* While he'd been obsessed with thoughts of her, she'd been regretting their experience. He began to wonder if it had just been a pity kiss, one designed to let him feel like a man again, since she'd called a halt to things when it had gotten a little too intense.

"Okay, I don't know what that look is, but I think you're getting the wrong idea."

"Really? What idea might that be?" Baldwin could feel his ire rising and tried to tamp down his irritation.

"I'm not really sure, but I'm sorry I was baiting you yesterday. That wasn't my intention."

"What was your intention then?"

"Hell, I don't know anymore. Sometimes I speak without thinking. I guess I was trying to get a rise out of you."

She'd certainly accomplished her goal, although probably not in the way she'd intended.

"So let me get this straight. You're apologizing for the disagreement?"

"Yes, of course. Wait a minute. What did you think I was apologizing for?"

"The disagreement."

"No, no, you thought I was apologizing for something to do with the kiss, didn't you?"

"Not at all." Although he'd been caught in the lie, it was kind of amusing to see her getting worked up over the issue. She stepped forward again, standing just at the edge of the pool. Her hands were now on her hips and her legs braced and ready for a fight, which only allowed him a better view up her skirt.

"Damn it, are you looking up my skirt again?" Kena gathered the material around her like a shield and bent down until she was almost at face level with him. "You are such a pervert."

"You're easily riled."

"I am not. I just don't understand how we can be having a serious conversation and the entire time you're more concerned about looking up my skirt."

He chuckled at her naivety. The reason was so obvious it hardly deserved an answer, but since she asked, "Because I'm a man?"

"You're infuriating is what you are."

"And you need to cool off." Reaching up, he grasped her upper arms and tugged, pulling her into the pool. He could see her eyes go wide with the realization of what was to come just as she hit the water. He moved toward the shallow end of the pool as she came up sputtering and wiping her wet hair out of her face.

"You. Are. A. Dead. Man."

Each word was enunciated distinctly. But instead of worry, Baldwin was too interested in noticing what the water had exposed. Her pink tank top was plastered to her skin and it was obvious she wasn't wearing a bra. Her nipples were puckered and poking through the damp material.

"Did you hear me? Dead. Man. Do you know how long it's going to take to flat iron my hair again?"

"Why would I know that?"

"Better question, why would you pull me into the pool? Something is seriously wrong with you."

"You think so." The madder she became, the harder he grew. Something was definitely wrong with him all right, because her fiery temper turned him on.

"I know so." She moved through the water until she was standing right in front of him. Her dark eyes were flashing with anger and her black hair lay like strands of seaweed. She was the epitome of a drowned rat, but it didn't detract from her beauty. He was beginning to believe nothing could.

"You're an insufferable ass. I'm going to kill you."

"But first you're going to kiss me."

He reached out and pulled her forcefully into his arms. Surprisingly she came willingly, grasping at his shoulders. Leaning down he captured her lips. She moaned and wrapped her arms around his neck as he slipped his tongue into her mouth.

The taste of Kena was as good as he'd remembered, hot and spicy with just a hint of sugar. Her tongue dueled with his as they kissed. Baldwin grasped her hips, bunching the material of her skirt in his hands. All he could think about was getting her out of her wet clothes so he could have access to her delectable skin.

With a quick yank he pulled the skirt over her hips and down past her thighs. She cooperated quite nicely by kicking her feet a few times, sending the skirt floating away. He broke their kiss and began nibbling down her neck, gently biting and then soothing her with a swipe of his tongue. At the same time she began to do some exploring of her own. Her free hand stroked down between them to touch his cock.

At the first touch of her hand, Baldwin moaned and thrust his hips in reaction, pressing his cock toward her questing fingers. He grasped the edge of her tank top and swiftly pulled it off, exposing her breasts to his gaze. The tips were like two dark brown berries, ones he was dying to taste. Taking advantage of the bountiful offering, he captured one of her turgid nipples in his mouth.

"Oh hell, yes."

"Like that do you? How about this?" Taking the hardened nub between his teeth Baldwin bit down.

Kena cried out in pleasure. "God, yes, I like it."

He chuckled again and then groaned as her hand clasped him tight. He pulled her hand away. "Enough of that or I won't be able to last."

"You know this is insanity."

He didn't mind going a little crazy if the result was a hot woman in his arms. "How so?"

"We barely know each other."

He pulled back to stare at her. The gentle lapping of the water was sending her pelvis rocking into his own with a steady rhythm.

"Do you want this?"

"Yes, I want you to fuck me."

"That's all I need to hear."

Turning her around, he pulled her body back, letting her feel his straining erection. He pinched her nipples, causing her to grind her ass against him. As he slipped his hands down her body, he tugged off her panties. Her legs fell open to allow him further access.

"Do you like me fingering your pussy?" He teased along her seam, never penetrating her, just continuing his soft stroking.

"More," she gasped. "Please, I need more."

"Like this?" He lightly grazed her clit, barely touching the engorged nub. She whimpered and arched her back to push her pussy against his hand.

"No, it's not enough."

"Tell me, tell me what you want."

"I want you inside me, please." She grabbed his hand and pressed it hard against her.

He pushed his finger inside, gently stroking her silken walls. His thumb grazed her sensitive bundle of nerves, causing her to jerk in reaction.

"God, yes, more, please."

Pressing a second and then third finger inside, he fucked her pussy with slow, even strokes, occasionally rubbing her clit. She voiced her appreciation with shallow gasps. As much as he loved hearing her breathy moans, he wanted her to come with his cock buried deep inside her. He pulled his hand from her warm pussy and she groaned in disappointment.

Moving them toward the cement steps, Baldwin ordered, "Kneel down, baby."

She knelt, her legs spread wide as the water lapped at her knees and with her ass thrust back toward him. Turning her head, she gave him a come-hither glance that left no questions as to her wants.

"Fuck me, Baldwin."

Ready to do her bidding, he quickly removed his trunks. Grasping his cock, he pushed into her warm, wet pussy. It was a very intense moment as her body opened to welcome him inside. He paused for a minute before pressing forward until she had fully taken his cock. Reaching around, he began to tease the nub at the apex of her thighs as he started the slow thrusting that would drive her crazy.

But Kena had other ideas. She began milking his cock almost as soon as he started fucking her, pushing him to the brink of insanity as he'd planned to do to her. He wouldn't last long at this rate. Trying to slow the pace wasn't helping either as she just continued to drive him over the edge.

"Stop playing games." Baldwin slapped her ass lightly causing her to jerk in surprise.

She whipped her head around and he could see desire blazing in her eyes. He wasn't sure if it was the slap or the sex, but at this point he didn't care.

"Who's playing games? You're deliberately torturing me here. No more teasing. Just fuck me. Fuck me hard and make me come."

Okay, who could turn down an order like that?

He pulled back until just the head of his cock was penetrating her pussy and then thrust forward with all his might. Arching her back in response, she grunted slightly, but pushed back against him, willing to give as much as she got. He began pistoning wildly, pounding into her pussy and pushing her forward with every plunge.

Reaching around in front of her, he pinched her clit, plucking at it fiercely as he continued his pounding. She was moaning incoherently, pushing back against him and crying out her impending orgasm.

"Come for me, baby. Come all over my cock." Baldwin pinched at her engorged nub steadily, never letting up on the pressure as her body convulsed around him.

Biting back his own need to come, he continued to thrust until she was limp from her orgasm before he withdrew and ejaculated on her back. He realized this was the first time since he was a teenager that he'd had sex with absolutely no protection. Gently lowering her into the water, he washed his semen off her back.

Although he would have liked to play the hero by picking her up and carrying her out of the pool, he knew it would be impossible. He could already feel the strain on his leg. He didn't want her desire to turn to pity when she realized his wound was bothering him, but realistically he knew there was no way he'd make it out of the pool without her assistance. It was just one more reason to add to the list of why he hated his injury.

Chapter Four

Kena felt boneless as she lay on the steps of the pool. The sex she'd just experienced had been mind blowing. Although she hadn't known for sure when she'd come over that the evening was going to end exactly like this, there had been that small thought in the back of her mind it might turn out this way. Otherwise why had she shaved before coming over to apologize?

"I don't think I can move."

"Neither do I."

While her statement was one of sexual exhaustion, the type people usually made in jest, she had a feeling his held a hint of truth in it. Looking over her shoulder she saw him grimace as if in pain.

"Are you okay?"

"I might need your help." She was surprised at his even tone. In fact, she was downright shocked he'd even voiced the words. She could tell asking her for help was the last thing he wanted to do, but she applauded his ability to do it nevertheless.

Kena struggled to her feet, bracing herself on the steps as she helped him rise. He leaned heavily on her as they slowly made their way up the steps toward the patio furniture.

"If you just help me to the chair you can go." There was a hint of bitterness in the tone of his voice.

She realized the man was in pain, but she wanted to smack him upside the head. She knew he probably just wanted to be left alone right now, but to her at least, his statement sounded like a dismissal. It was bad enough when all she was trying to do was help him. But to do it right after they had wild, crazy pool sex, that was going too far. Deciding to just ignore him for the moment, she lowered him into the nearest chair.

"I'm going to find your medicine."

"No, it's fine. I'll just sit here for a minute. Don't bother." His words were polite enough, but the meaning was clear. He didn't want her to see him in pain, but that was too damned bad.

"I'm not going to argue; why don't you just tell me where the pills are so I don't have to tear the house apart?"

Baldwin tried to stare her down, but his pain-filled eyes weren't up to the task. He finally nodded his head briefly. "Master bathroom cabinet, top shelf."

Before he could change his mind, she darted into the house. When she opened the patio door, she gasped in shock at the cold air hitting her wet, naked body. With care she sprinted up the stairs, praying to every deity known to man that she wouldn't slip on the floor and break her neck. When she made it to the bedroom, she dashed across the room to the bathroom. Flipping on the light, she quickly opened the medicine cabinet and located the elusive pain pills. Thankfully, he hadn't thrown them out.

In the kitchen, she filled a glass with water then hurried back out to his side. Baldwin's mouth was tight and although she knew the man was white, he looked even paler than should be normal. His hand was unconsciously rubbing at his injured leg. Even his breathing seemed a bit off.

"Here, take them."

Instead of arguing, he wordlessly accepted the pills and quickly swallowed them with the water before leaning back in the chair and closing his eyes. Kena knew he must really be hurting if he wasn't even willing to bicker. Feeling helpless, she took the glass from his hand and headed back indoors.

Shaking her head in disgust, she noted the kitchen looked worse for wear because of her early departure the day before. It would have to go both first and last on her things to do tomorrow. Kena ran back up the stairs, thanking the good Lord she'd started a recent step aerobics class. Otherwise all the exercise she was getting tonight most likely would have killed her.

She scoured through his dresser drawers and found a T-shirt and shorts that didn't look too ridiculous on her and quickly dressed. Then she pulled his robe off the hook in the bathroom and headed back downstairs. As she returned to the backyard, Baldwin opened one eye at her arrival.

"You can leave, you know."

"Yeah, I know. You've already tried to send me packing once. When you can do it yourself, then maybe we'll talk about it. Until then, just shut up and let me help get you into bed."

A small smile flitted over his lips. "Wasn't it me trying to get you into bed that got us into this mess?"

"Hardy har har." She took his hands in hers and tugged him to his feet. "You need to put this on."

"Why? I'm just going to bed."

"Because, once you open the door you're going to realize how damn cold it is in your house, especially coming in naked from the pool. You need to be covered and dried off before you go to bed."

"Yes, Mother," he intoned sarcastically.

"Hey now, no reason to insult me," she teased back as Baldwin snorted.

She wrapped her arms around his waist and they slowly made their way into the house. Getting up the stairs was a chore to say the least. They had to pause a number of times, and even sat down to rest for a moment when they hit the landing. Finally reaching the master bedroom, she herded him toward the bathroom instead of allowing him to lie down on the bed.

She flipped down the lid on the toilet and gestured for him to sit. When he complied, she grabbed the towel off the rack and began to dry his hair.

"You know, I'm not a child. I can do it myself." He tried to grab the towel away from her, but Kena stepped back and held it out of reach. She wasn't going to argue with him about it. Instead she was arbitrarily taking over, whether he liked it or not. He obviously didn't, but that was too damned bad.

"When you can sit by yourself without falling over and dry off each one of your toes, maybe I'll think about it. Until then, leave well enough alone."

"You're a lot more bossy than you have a right to be."

"When you're feeling better, you can do something about it. I'll be looking forward to the confrontation."

Although she hadn't noticed it so much the other day, his hair was a bit longer than it should have been for a military cut. There was actually a small bit hanging down over his forehead she wanted to push back. Unfortunately, she had a feeling he'd consider it more coddling.

Rather than linger over taking care of him, which he seemed to consider a burden to her, Kena tried to quickly and efficiently towel him down. Slipping the robe off his shoulder, she stifled the gasp at seeing him nude. Even though she had made love with him only moments earlier, the sight of his tightly honed body took her breath away. Damn, he looked hot, even now. She was reacting to the fact she was able to touch him so intimately, even if he wasn't feeling well.

And he was responding accordingly. His cock began to rise and by the time she was kneeling at his feet she almost had to stop herself from taking him into her mouth. Only the reminder that he was fading fast and looked ready to pass out at any moment put a stop to her errant fantasies.

He must have felt the mutual frustration as well because he finally pulled the towel from her hands and threw it down. "Thanks, I think we're done here. Just help me to bed."

His begrudging thank you was a bit brusque, but she had feeling it was sincere as well. Helping him to his feet, she wrapped her arms around him once again. Baldwin was leaning even more heavily against her and she realized his pain medication had finally started to do its job. Realistically, however, it meant she needed to get him to bed as quickly as possible before he passed out.

When they reached the bed, Kena pulled back the comforter and sheet and helped him sit. He took a deep breath, as if he were going to say something, but then just swung his legs onto the bed. He laid back, arm thrown over his eyes as if needing to block out all light. Kena pulled the covers over him.

"Do you need anything else?" She waited for a moment, but hearing no answer wondered if the pain meds had already put him to sleep. She returned to the bathroom and cleaned up before flipping off the light.

When she walked back into the bedroom, she had to stop for a moment to let her eyes adjust to the dark. At first she didn't know if she was hearing something, but then realized it was Baldwin speaking softly, finally answering her earlier question.

"Only you can give me what I want."

Walking back toward him, she sat on the edge of the bed. "What is it? What do you need?"

"You."

Shocked, she stared at him. His words had begun to slur and she wondered if he even realized he'd spoken aloud. His hand reached out and clasped hers and Kena knew her decision now could be a life-altering one. She could just pull away and leave as planned. Baldwin most likely wouldn't remember this incident and even if he did would probably pretend it never happened.

On the other hand she could throw caution to the wind and stay. She could get to know this man she'd just let into her body and figure out if there was something to this thing she felt between them. Knowing there was only one decision to make, she pulled back the covers and climbed into bed beside him.

She might wake up in the morning to find she'd made a horrible mistake, but somehow she didn't think so.

* * *

Baldwin awoke to the sounds of activity coming from the kitchen. For the first time since he'd been injured he hadn't been woken by nightmares haunting his sleep. And to top it off, although his leg ached, it didn't feel as bad as he'd anticipated. He hated to admit it, but it could have something to do with taking the pain medication, which he'd been refusing to do ninety percent of the time.

Turning his head, he noticed a slight indentation in the pillow next to him. Kena had spent the night. He waited for that sinking feeling, knowing he never liked having a woman sleep over, but it never came.

He remembered pulling her into the pool and the mind-blowing sex that followed. He even recalled the humiliating period after, where she had to practically drag him from the pool and up the stairs in order to get him into bed.

But he couldn't remember asking her to stay. In fact, he had a vague recollection he'd actually told her she could go. Thankfully, she'd ignored his directive; otherwise he might still be sitting naked on the patio this morning.

He still didn't know how he was going to react to seeing her though. She'd seen him at his most vulnerable. He hated the idea he would look weak in her eyes. He didn't need or want her pity.

Sitting up, Baldwin swung his legs around until they hung off the bed. Although his leg didn't feel the worst it ever had, this morning wasn't exactly a picnic. He gritted his teeth, psyching himself up for the trek across the room. After a few minutes he decided to just to go for it, and painstakingly made his way to the bathroom.

After a hot, steaming shower he almost felt normal. Almost being the operative word. The heat had loosened the tightened muscles in his leg somewhat so he wasn't walking with the stiffened gait he had earlier. But the deep throbbing was ever present. He reluctantly grabbed the pill bottle and swallowed half the dosage. As he gingerly dressed, he wondered if he would ever heal.

Heading down the stairs he could hear Kena singing slightly off key, but with a lot of energy and enthusiasm. As he approached the kitchen he was amazed at the sight that greeted him.

She had found an old scarf from his room and wrapped it around her head and was wearing an oversized T-shirt and a pair of boxer shorts that practically fell off her ass, but she looked remarkable. Her face was glowing as she sang along to the music playing through her earbuds. Finally noticing him standing in the door, she smiled as she came to a halt and turned off the headset.

"Good morning. I hope my cleaning didn't wake you."

She looked entirely too cheerful this morning, which pissed him off since he wasn't exactly a morning person. In addition, he wasn't too sure how he felt about her being here after last night. On the one hand, the sex had been amazing. Kena had responded to him like no other woman had in a long time. It even made him wonder if she'd be responsive to some of his darker desires.

On the other hand, he'd gone from being on top of the world to the lowest low. And she'd been there to witness the fall. Not only witnessed it, but picked up the pieces. He didn't want to need anyone. Despite being attracted to her, he didn't want to need her. Baldwin wanted to stand on his own two feet, figuratively and literally.

"Actually, it did." He headed toward the coffeepot to pour himself a cup, forcing himself to walk as normally as possible and not show any weakness. "Don't you think it's a bit early in the morning for all this?"

"I usually start at nine o'clock and it's already ten, so no, this isn't early."

"I suppose my mother set up that schedule."

"Actually, it's my normal schedule, but yes, she approved it."

"If you're going to stay on, we've got to make some changes."

Before she could ask exactly what those might entail, a knock on the French doors interrupted them. Before he could answer it, the door swung open and Gloria popped her head inside.

"Oh good, you're up. I was hoping you would be." She bounded into the room and greeted him with a kiss. He turned his head so her lips hit his cheek instead of her intended target. "I came in through the backyard to see if you had started your laps."

He knew his parents were trying to foster something between the two of them, but this was getting ridiculous. "What are you doing here?"

"Is that any kind of greeting? I came over to help cheer you on while you did your laps this morning. I missed coming over yesterday."

"No one invited you to be my cheerleader." Although he spoke to the blonde, his gaze was fixed on Kena's back, shaking with laughter as she stood at the sink. She must be remembering her mockery of the overly cheerful woman from the day before, just as he had.

Gloria pouted in disappointment. "Aww, I thought you enjoyed my visits."

"Not particularly."

Gloria just laughed and smacked him lightly on the arm. "Silly, you don't mean that. You're just being an old stick-in-the-mud. Once you get all healed up we'll have lots of fun together."

He didn't want to hurt her feelings, but there was no chance in hell he'd ever consider her as a girlfriend. He needed to get her out of there. Her presence was getting on his nerves. Although he didn't realize it before, her voice was a bit too grating, reminding him of someone who'd sucked helium before they talked. Every time she came over the only thing they talked about was his injury. It was getting old really fast.

"Baldwin, are you listening to me?" Her eyes narrowed a bit as she stared at him. Baldwin dragged his gaze away from Kena so he could concentrate on the problem at hand.

"Yeah, of course." He'd heard everything she'd said, he just didn't care about it.

Gloria turned her gaze to Kena, who was finishing loading the dishwasher.

"This must be the new maid your mother was telling me about. Interesting work attire," she noted, addressing herself to Kena.

Kena turned and smiled, but somehow the look didn't quite reach her eyes. "I make it a policy to work in comfortable clothing."

Gloria eyed her up and down. "Comfortable is one thing, but I must say you won't be viewed very professionally wearing an outfit that looks as if you slept in it."

Since she most likely had slept in the clothes, Gloria wasn't too far off the mark. Baldwin started to chuckle at the irony but quickly turned it into a cough when Gloria glanced his way.

"It's a good thing I don't strive for your approval then."

Gloria studied her freshly manicured nails for a moment before eying Kena once again. "You know, I've been thinking about hiring a house girl for my condo. With all my volunteering, I just don't have the time to devote to all these little mundane tasks."

House girl. Now that was going a bit too far, but before he could intervene, Kena spoke up.

"It's too bad really, but you can't afford me." She sent Gloria a little smirk before sauntering from the room.

"How dare she speak to me in such a rude manner? I've never been treated so shabbily in all my life."

He somehow doubted that. Gloria had a reputation for treating service staff with total disregard. However, he didn't think she'd appreciate it if he pointed that out to her.

"Someone should talk to her." Gloria turned as if she was going to follow Kena, but he grabbed her arm, stopping her in mid-motion. He wanted her gone, not wandering through the house where it might take him hours to get rid of her instead of minutes.

"You know, you're right. Someone should talk to her." With his hand on her elbow he began to guide her toward the door. "I'm going to do that right now."

"Well if you think that's best." She looked confused, as if she didn't know why her visit had turned around so quickly.

"I do. Good-bye." Although he didn't literally shove her out the door, it was a close call. Of course she would probably run right over to his parents' house to complain of his treatment of her and he'd be subjected to another phone call from his dad. But he just didn't care. His parents might have gotten him to succumb to their power play once before, but he wasn't giving in as easily this time.

Chapter Five

As she stood in the upstairs hallway, pretending to put items away in the linen closet, Kena could overhear the entire conversation between Baldwin and Gloria. The man was an equal opportunity grump, being just as rude to Gloria as he'd been to her the other day. Although she had a feeling Gloria hadn't been treated to his better side. The one she'd had sex with in the pool.

Just remembering last night made her squeeze her thighs together. The thought of fucking him was unbelievable, in more ways than one. Although he was one of the best lovers she'd ever had, she was still wondering why she'd had sex with him in the first place.

One-night stands weren't exactly her style. Neither was having sex with someone after speaking to them exactly twice. Hell, she wasn't even dating him. Kena wasn't a prude, but she could count on one hand the number of men she'd slept with and all of them had been during a long-term relationship.

This situation with him threw her into completely unknown territory. When she woke up this morning, she had to fight with her instinct to wrap her arms around his body, somehow knowing it wouldn't be appreciated by him in the light of day. She wasn't an idiot and she realized he had issues with his injury and any hint of appearing incapable in front of others. Personally she couldn't figure it out, but men could be very particular about any sign of weakness and Baldwin seemed to have inherited that gene in spades.

Instead of snuggling like she had wanted, she'd slipped out of bed only to discover about a billion messages left on her cell phone by her aunt. It had taken some fancy footwork to smooth the rough edges down, but in the end, her aunt reluctantly forgave her. Not for the one-night stand, because she was a grown ass woman, but for her not being courteous enough to call.

Shaking herself from her daydreaming, Kena realized she could no longer hear voices from downstairs. He must have gotten rid of her, because she didn't figure the other woman was the type who could shut up for very long. As if she conjured him from her thoughts alone, she caught a movement out of the corner of her eye. He had turned the corner and was beginning to make his way up the stairs.

She figured he wouldn't want her to stand around watching as he struggled with the steps so she quickly finishing up in the linen closet and headed into his bedroom to make the bed. She had just fluffed the final pillow when she looked up to find him standing in the doorway staring at her.

"What are you doing?"

She thought it was pretty obvious, but okay, she'd play his game. "Making the bed."

"You don't have to do that."

"Yes I do. I'm the housekeeper. I clean things and make the beds. It's actually part of my job description."

"We need to talk. Let's go to my office."

Resisting the urge to salute, she rolled her eyes and followed him from the bedroom. She felt as if she were headed to the principal's office. His office was at the end of the hallway and it looked like it hadn't been updated since his grandfather owned the home. The walls were lined with bookshelves that were mostly empty when she'd first opened the house and dusted in here. Now, however, the floor was covered in boxes that looked like they needed to be unpacked.

Once inside, Baldwin sat heavily on the chair behind the desk while she sat across from him. She knew the walk had tired him out, but he was still pretending his leg didn't hurt. The man was a menace to his own health and well-being.

"You can't keep working here."

Well damn. That was straightforward and to the point.

"Why?"

"I don't think it's appropriate for me to be sleeping with the person cleaning my home."

Biting back her initial retort, she just stared at him for a moment. His comment could be taken so many ways, most of them not good. She didn't think he was saying he was too good for her. In fact, it almost felt as if the opposite were true. On the other hand this wasn't turning out to be the best morning-after conversation she'd ever had.

"You know, sleeping with the boss usually helps you move up the company ladder, not get fired."

"There is no company ladder and I'm not the boss. Besides, I don't need a housekeeper."

Kena mentally shook her head. The man had a real problem with money. God forbid she ever had such issues.

"Hey, you're right. You're not the boss. Your mom hired me and she'll have to be the one to fire me." She crossed her arms and smiled, settling back into her chair. "As far as needing a housekeeper, haven't we already had that conversation?"

"I don't appreciate your attitude."

"I don't appreciate your grouchiness, but we all have our crosses to bear."

"Your mouth is going to get you into trouble. Gloria was ready to give you a piece of her mind after your conversation in the kitchen."

"She can't afford to lose any more brain cells, so I think I'll pass."

"So true, she can't at that." Baldwin looked like he wanted to laugh, but was deliberately suppressing the urge. It was the only time she'd seen him loosen up even a little bit except for last night in the pool, when they'd had sex.

Nope, I can't think about that now.

"She was deliberately trying to insult me. She's a spoiled, rich brat and she got exactly what she deserved."

"I thought you wanted jobs from my mother's friends and associates."

"After our conversation, I've revised my thoughts on that subject. I think I can live without the hassle."

"If I told my mother some of the insults you threw around about her friends she'd fire you so fast your head would be spinning."

"But you won't."

He frowned, obviously perturbed she could read him so well and that he wasn't going to be able to get his way. "I don't want you here so why would you want to stay?"

"Just a masochist, I guess." She wasn't willing to go away so easily. She was agreeable to be laid back about the whole thing, but she really was intrigued by this man, despite all his foibles. "Besides, you haven't seen my French-maid outfit yet."

His eyes flared for a brief moment before he lowered his gaze. "That's a perfect example of one of our problems."

She decided to file away his devilish glance as something to be examined at a later date and concentrated on his words instead. "Okay, I'm confused. Can you explain it to the rest of the class?"

"If you're going to stay, we have to set some ground rules."

"Such as?"

"You have too many smart aleck comebacks. Aren't maids supposed to be seen and not heard?"

"I think that applies to children, not maids. When did it become okay to tell the black girl she wasn't allowed to speak?"

"I didn't say you couldn't speak, just that I didn't need to hear your ongoing commentary. It's annoying."

"Too bad. I say what I think."

"Keep it to yourself."

Kena pursed her lips and didn't respond. If he wanted to think she was agreeing, then fine. She'd continue to say exactly what was on her mind when she felt like it. "Anything else?"

"I like my mornings quiet. You need to come by later in the day."

"I can't do that. I have a schedule to maintain. In fact, I need to leave here soon to get to my afternoon job today."

"Change your schedule and do my house in the afternoons or find another job."

He was deliberately trying to get her to quit, but it wasn't going to work. "I'll speak with my afternoon clients today and see if they're willing to be flexible and make a change."

"There are some other schedule changes you can make as well. I don't need someone here three days."

"It's only three half days and as long as you're still getting settled, I think you do. Take this room, for example. All this stuff needs to be organized and put away, which is something I can do."

He looked around the room reluctantly. "Fine, until I get settled then. But this is a point we'll be renegotiating."

"Fine, we'll discuss it again later." She stood up, ready to leave. "Are we done, because I need to get back to work?"

"No, we are not done. Sit back down."

She grimaced and flopped back into her chair. "Come on, just how many useless rules do you have?"

"Only one more. There won't be any more slips like last night. We can't sleep together if you continue to work here. This is a professional relationship only."

She was stuck in the proverbial Catch-22 situation. If she stayed, no more nookie, but if she left, she most likely wouldn't see him and therefore wouldn't be able to get to know him better. Weighing her choices carefully she decided to play devil's advocate. She knew he didn't want her to stay and she also wanted to make sure she got to know him better.

"I think I can suffer the consequences." Kena figured she'd just have to find a way to change his mind.

Baldwin watched through hooded eyes as Kena left the room. Their discussion didn't go exactly as he'd planned. In fact, he had the feeling she was laughing at him under all her supposed agreement. The sad fact was she made him feel something he'd been suppressing since he'd returned home from the war. Her presence was a temptation he couldn't afford.

Unfortunately, now that he had tasted her, he only wanted more. Just remembering the feel of her soft skin had him hardening. Her responsiveness last night almost made him regret pushing her away. But he'd laid down his rules and she'd agreed, almost eagerly.

It doesn't matter.

Pushing away from the desk, he looked at the boxes that were piled around the room. She'd been right about this mess. Some of these boxes dated back to his high school and college days. Having someone around to help him get everything organized and put away would be a blessing. Of course that would mean they would be working even closer with each other.

He had to stop these wayward thoughts and complete his plan to regain his health instead of daydreaming about a woman he had no right to be thinking about. It was hard to ignore her, though, when he glanced up again to find her standing in the doorway, still wearing the boxer shorts and T-shirt she'd appropriated from him.

He glanced at his watch. "Are you leaving?"

"Missing me already?"

"Hardly."

Kena picked at the hem of the T-shirt. "I just wanted to say I'll be washing these and returning them Friday when I come back."

"We'll get started on this room then."

"Ooo, can't wait." Her false enthusiasm was obvious. She turned and left the office and he could hear her moving through the house before she left. He finally released the pent-up breath he'd been holding. He'd been right to worry about her presence. Even with her agreement to keep things professional, he wondered how long *he'd* be able to resist her.

Trying to push thoughts of Kena from him, he booted up his computer and tried to lose himself in work. It was a futile effort, however, when he was interrupted less than twenty minutes later by the sound of his mother's voice.

"Yoo-hoo. Baldwin. It's your mother. I've come for a visit."

Dropping his head into his hands, he groaned in despair of their upcoming discussion. His mother never stopped by without an ulterior motive. He tried to avoid confrontations with her at all costs.

He and his parents never saw eye to eye. If he wasn't the spitting image of them he'd almost think he'd been adopted. Thankfully he'd taken after his grandfather, a self-made man who made no bones of the fact he didn't appreciate his own daughter's avarice.

At the knock on his office door, he raised his head to see his mother standing in the doorway.

"Why are you hiding up here?" She entered the room and sat primly down in the chair Kena had vacated earlier.

"I was working on the computer, Mother. Since I wasn't expecting guests, I didn't know I should be downstairs ready to receive."

"There's no need to be rude."

Baldwin wasn't going to apologize so he jumped right to the point. "To what do I owe the pleasure of this visit?"

"I swear, Baldwin, I thought I raised you better than this. You speak so harshly to everyone. You were never like this as a boy. Once you went to high school and started hanging out with those hoodlum friends of yours you completely changed."

He shook his head at the long-standing argument. He'd heard it most of his adult life. She didn't like his friends and she didn't like most of the choices he made in his life. Nevertheless, he should have known better than to push his mother. She always did everything in her own timeframe and wouldn't allow her agenda to be altered.

"Mother, I'm tired and I don't have time for this. You obviously came here for a reason. Can we cut to the chase?"

"Are you telling me your mother can't stop by to see you? My God, Baldwin, you almost died. Do you think I'm totally heartless? Your father and I love you and I wanted to make sure you're okay."

He knew he should be more grateful. After he was injured he'd been hospitalized overseas before being transferred back to the United States. Although the VA hospital did the best they could, it wasn't the most pleasant experience. Once he was back in the country, his parents used all their wealth and power to make sure he was in the best private rehabilitation hospital and had the best doctors.

He was sure his care was far and above what most soldiers had received. And instead of being pleased by it, he was filled with shame and guilt because he'd taken advantage of everything his parents offered to him even though in the past he'd always shunned their wealth. He knew they did love him, in their own way. The problem was they couldn't comprehend how different his ideals were from their own.

"My rehabilitation is coming along fine. There's no need to worry."

Sitting back in her chair, his mother eyed him speculatively. "Gloria had a lot to say about that."

That pain in the ass socialite was really becoming a thorn in his side. "What would she have to say about anything? She's not my doctor or physical therapist. Hell, she doesn't even work in the medical field."

"Just because she's not a medical expert doesn't mean she can't be concerned. She's a lovely girl. Her mother is head of the docents at the museum."

As if he cared what her mother did in her spare time? The only reason his mother cared was because she was determined to marry him off, especially to the right kind of girl. The one whose family would garner her the social connections she strived for.

"Mother, I'm not interested in her concerns. Hell, I'm not interested in her, period."

Ignoring his words, she continued to rant. "She told me you've been acting oddly, that you practically threw her out this morning."

"She deserved it, showing up here unannounced and uninvited. As for me acting oddly, how would she know what was odd for me? We haven't seen each other in years."

"You want to know what's odd? How about you ignoring a beautiful, well-respected young lady to swim naked in the pool with the cleaning woman?"

Son of a bitch. Just one more problem he didn't need.

She crossed her arms as if in triumph. How Gloria found out about Kena and the pool he had no idea. She had obviously immediately run to tattle to his mother, probably hoping she would bring him into line. The problem was she didn't realize he wouldn't acquiesce to his mother and he wasn't ashamed of being with Kena. In fact, if it meant getting rid of the pain in the ass debutante, he'd flaunt Kena from the rooftops.

"Speaking of which, whoever asked you to hire me a cleaning service?"

Her face fell at his words. "I just thought it would be a nice gesture. And I hired a minority. Not that I hired a black girl just because they're good at cleaning. She was the cheapest."

Unbelievable. His mother's outdated stereotypes and subtle attempts to be politically correct while insulting those she pretended to be supporting were a joke.

"Kena is a beautiful, intelligent young woman who owns her own business and has a head on her shoulders, which is more than I can say for your little protégé. It's none of her business who I decide to spend my time with or how I spend my time. In fact, it's none of your business either."

She stood in a fury, hands on her hips. "I can't believe you. How dare you put that woman on the same level as Gloria? What did I ever do to deserve such an ungrateful child?"

"Stop being so melodramatic, Mother." He sighed. Why did every get-together have to be so damn trying?

"You'll eventually come to your senses and realize what a terrible mistake you've made. I can only hope Gloria will still be around." She flounced from the room in a huff.

Baldwin shook his head in amazement. He could speak, but she just wouldn't or couldn't comprehend him. It was no use arguing with her when she was like this. She'd eventually realize he'd never be the son she wanted him to be.

Chapter Six

Your services are no longer required.

Kena hit stop, rewind, and then play again to listen to the entire message again.

Ms. Rutherford, this is Mrs. Garrett. After speaking to my son today, please consider this phone call official notification...

"Kena, are you listening to that message *again?*"

Kena hit the stop button and looked up to find her aunt standing in the doorway of her office. She had turned a small room in the back of the house into her official office for TLC. It had a separate entrance, and since she didn't need to rent out an actual office space just yet it worked out well. Someday she might be as big as Merry Maids, but she wasn't there yet.

"I can't help it. I keep listening to try and hear if I can figure out if I'm missing something."

"What could you be missing? The woman fired you, end of story."

Kena couldn't refute her words. She'd been fired. After agreeing to all of Baldwin's stupid ground rules, his mother called and fired her anyway. She was so mad she could spit nails. He was a coward, plain and simple.

"I can see the wheels turning. What are you thinking?"

"This is all his fault, the evil bastard. How dare he whine to his mother to get rid of me instead of confronting me himself?"

"I think you're assuming an awful lot. Have you talked to him yourself to get his side of the story?"

"There is no his side of the story."

Her aunt shook her head. "You're cutting off your nose to spite your face. Instead of pouting and sulking you ought to be talking to the man."

"I already went to his house and apologized after our last argument and you know where that led. I'm done going over there and being the humble one. I'm the injured party here."

"I know better than to argue with you. You'll do what you want. Just remember, I'm here with a shoulder to cry on if you need me."

Kena smiled. "Thanks, but it won't be necessary. There are no tears here. I'm angry, not sad."

The phone rang and her aunt chuckled as she headed back toward the house.

"TLC, how may I help you?"

"It's Friday; where the hell are you?"

No he did not. Baldwin calling her? Impossible. The man was completely insane.

"I don't work for you anymore."

"You left here Wednesday saying you'd be back Friday. What changed your mind?"

She couldn't believe his gall. He was blaming her? Crazy bastard. "You did, when you had your mother fire me."

Slamming down the phone she felt better than she had all morning. Almost immediately the phone began ringing. She had no illusions it was anyone other than Baldwin. Rather than answer it she turned off the ringer, letting the call go to her answering machine. She was more than willing to possibly lose some business instead of having to listen to any more of his bullshit.

She tried to clear her mind of all the negative energy of the morning and work on the accounting reports. Unfortunately her mind wouldn't stay on task and she found her thoughts drifting to her conversations with Baldwin. Although he could be rude, she got the impression he was honest almost to a fault. That's why she'd been so shocked by his betrayal.

Mulling over her aunt's words, she wondered if she'd misjudged him. She wanted to believe he had nothing to do with it, but what other reason would his mother have to fire her. The only logical explanation was Baldwin. The sad thing was how disappointed she felt. She thought they had come to some sort of understanding.

Once again she tried to return to work, burying her head in numbers before her tactic proved futile. Sitting back in her chair she massaged her temples, trying to abate the headache that was threatening to explode inside her head.

She should just go lie down and try to sleep the pain away since she wasn't really getting any work completed.

"You look about like how I feel."

Kena slowly raised her head to find Baldwin standing in the doorway to her office. Not only had the man gotten her fired, now he was insulting her if she understood him correctly. Why did he look so damned attractive? Her body might be reacting favorably to him, but she wasn't going to allow her brain to betray her as well.

"Why are you here?"

"I think we need to talk."

"No, I think you need to leave. I no longer work for you and I don't have to obey you anymore."

"When did you ever," Baldwin muttered as he pulled out a chair from the corner of the room and made himself at home.

"How dare you. You set the ground rules and I agreed to abide by them. I wasn't the one who reneged on the deal."

"Neither did I."

"Really?" She didn't know why he was backpedaling now, but she had his mother's voice on tape, she didn't need anything else to prove her point.

"Yes, really. I don't know what you think I did, but I had nothing to do with anything my mother might have said or done."

"What I think? You are too much, you know that? I don't lie and I can prove exactly what your mother said." Leaning forward she pressed the play button on the answering machine.

Ms. Rutherford, this is Mrs. Garrett. After speaking to my son today, please consider this phone call official notification that your services are no longer required.

"I believe that says it all." Kena didn't want to feel vindicated, but she did. The man needed to own up to what happened.

"Not quite. Obviously my mother did fire you --"

"Obviously."

"However, I had nothing to do with it. I don't lie either, by the way. And no matter what she says, I didn't ask her to fire you."

"What other reason would she have to fire me? I did an excellent job at your house, so it can't be the quality of work. Besides, she said she spoke with you."

"She did speak with me, but on an entirely different subject." Baldwin ran his fingers through his hair. "Unfortunately, I don't think you'll like what she actually said anymore than what you think was said."

"Why don't you spit it out?"

"She showed up Wednesday after you left and told me Gloria had told her about our tryst in the pool."

"I-I don't understand. How did Gloria --"

"Before you jump to conclusions, no, I didn't tell her anything. I have no idea how she found out. She came to visit, bitched at me, and I basically told her to mind her own business. At no time did I ask her to fire you."

"If you knew about this since Wednesday, why didn't you tell me?"

"For one thing I had no idea she was going fire you. For another, I was never going to tell you. What good would it have done?"

"Because I might want to know my name is being thrown around as slut of the month?"

"That's not going to happen. My mother would never tell anyone. It might reflect poorly on her. Just imagine the horror. Her son sleeping with the black help."

"What about Gloria?"

"I have no idea." Baldwin had the audacity to look confused, as if he'd never considered the blonde bimbo might open her trap.

"Just like a man. You have no idea. I don't need that bitch telling everyone I'm a ho who sleeps with her clients."

"I'll talk to her."

"Don't do me any favors." Kena pushed away from her desk and stood up.

"Maybe I'm doing myself one."

"Or maybe if you would have stood up to your mother a long time ago none of this would be happening."

"Right." He stood as well, his eyes alive with anger. "And if my mother hadn't been the nosy busybody that she is, you would have never been hired and we would have never fucked."

"You say that like it's a bad thing." She was beginning to think meeting him might have been the worst thing that had happened to her.

"You think it is."

Kena stared at him incredulously. Would wonders never cease? "Weren't you the same man who told me in no uncertain terms we weren't going to sleep together again?"

"Yes."

"Then why the hell would I think fucking you was a good thing?"

"Because it was fucking fantastic."

It had been better than that but she would never admit it. "Says you."

"And you, when you screamed my name as you came."

"Whatever it is or was, it's now over." Kena walked over and opened the door. "I think you should leave."

Stalking to the door, he pushed it shut and slammed her back against the hard wood. "It's over when I say it's over."

Her eyes widened as he bent his head and captured her lips in a punishing kiss. His tongue swept inside her mouth, dueling with her own for power and control. She felt as if she were in a maelstrom, caught between the unyielding door behind her and the hard-as-nails man pressing in front of her. And she loved every minute of it.

Baldwin continued to find himself totally captivated by this woman. Her fire and passion for life seemed to awaken something in him he'd thought long dead. He'd come to see her to straighten out the misunderstanding about her job, but all he could think about was kissing those lips, stripping her bare to expose her soft dark skin, and possessing her in the most intimate way.

When she'd asked him to leave, he decided there was no way in hell he was going to let her go. He knew he wasn't thinking logically. In fact, he'd been the one to insist they not sleep together again. But when it was all said and done, he couldn't get her out of his mind. He wanted to hear her admit it was as good as he knew it was.

He'd expected some resistance to his bulldozing tactics. Instead, after a brief moment's hesitation she met his kiss with a fiery intensity of her own. He gripped her hips fiercely as he pressed against her, wanting her to feel his overpowering need. Her fingers were gripping his jacket lapels as they kissed and her hips continued to shift in subtle reaction, spurring on his own response.

Moving one hand from her hip, he pulled her shirt free of her jeans and swept upward, caressing the smooth expanse of skin until he reached her bra. With deft fingers he unhooked the garment, releasing her breasts.

His other hand stroked over her belly before moving ever upward. Breaking their kiss for a moment, he ordered, "Lift your arms." She obeyed instantly and he swept her shirt and bra off in one swift movement, tossing them aside. Her breasts were firm and high, just ready for him to taste.

Bending his head, he circled her nipple with his tongue before sucking it into his mouth. Kena moaned, her head pressed back against the door as he continued to suckle at her breast. He began to nibble and nip at the tip and she gasped in reaction.

"Shit, that hurts."

"Good hurt or bad hurt?"

Kena was silent for so long Baldwin decided to remind her about what she was deciding and bit down on the hard nub. Her body shuddered in response as she finally answered. "Good hurt."

He chuckled and transferred his attention to her other breast, treating it with the same loving care. His bites were obviously arousing her as she continued to moan and rub herself against his cloth-covered cock.

"You get off on the rougher stuff, don't you?"

"Maybe I do."

Cupping her breasts, he took each of her nipples between finger and thumb and squeezed hard. She keened her pleasure, biting her lip in an apparently futile effort to keep quiet.

"No maybe about it, baby. You love rough nipple play and maybe even more."

She shivered in his arms as he continued to pinch and pull the sensitive tips of her breasts. "I like what you're doing, yes. As for more, I don't know."

"Hmm, I guess we'll just have to see." Stepping back for a moment, he stared intently at her. "Strip down and let me see that sweet pussy of yours."

"What about you? I don't want to be the only one standing here with no clothes on."

"No worries, we'll both be naked soon enough."

While she watched, he stripped off his jacket and shirt in record time. He toed off his shoes and then shimmied out of his trousers before seating himself in his previously vacated chair. He took his cock in hand, stroking along the hard shaft as he watched her strip down for him.

Kena was a sight to behold, an ebony goddess. She kicked off her heels and then turning her back to him, she quickly unbuttoned her jeans and pushed them down over her hips, revealing a red thong. The cocoa-colored skin of her ass looked good enough to eat and he imagined what she might do if he leaned forward to take a bite.

Pushing her jeans off her legs, she kicked them away before turning back around. She hooked her fingers into the sides of the thong, pulling the scrap of material down with interminable slowness. He watched her reveal her pussy to his hungry gaze. As much as he wanted to taste her, he also wanted to bury himself deep inside her.

"Like what you see?"

She spread her legs slightly and he groaned at the sight of her light mocha lips glistening with her dew.

"Hell yes."

Reaching out he stroked along her seam, his finger briefly dipping inside, before bringing his hand back to his mouth. Licking his fingers, he groaned again at the sweet and spicy taste.

"I want you inside me." Kena's voice was husky and low.

"I want that too, but we need a condom." Before he could grab his pants and dig out his wallet, she dropped to the floor and found it first. She quickly discovered the foil packet inside and ripped it open, letting the leather wallet dropped from her hands.

Leaning forward she swiped her tongue over the tip of his cock teasingly before rolling the latex sheath down.

"Ride me, baby."

Needing no further urging, she straddled him. She grasped his cock in her hands, but instead of immediately sinking onto him, she teased some more, rubbing her pussy along his throbbing length and grinding her clit against his hardness.

Being that close to heaven was maddening. "Enough."

Baldwin wrapped his hand over hers and guided his cock to her entrance. He thrust forward as she pushed down, sinking into her honey depths. Her fingers dug into his shoulders as she continued to lower herself over him until he was finally balls deep inside her.

"You're so deep. I feel so full."

Her words were like licks of flame up his spine. He wanted to pound into her, no holds barred. But instead he held her hips tightly as he tried to maintain his fragile control.

"Move, baby. Show me."

Closing her eyes, she grasped his shoulders to steady herself as she began to rock back and forth slowly. Baldwin returned his attention to her breasts, his fingers grazing her pebbled nipples. Her movements began to increase in tempo at his every touch. She released a shuddering breath and he could feel her nails digging into his shoulders as she continued to ride him.

Finally releasing her breasts, he zeroed in on her clit, encouraging her every movement. He strummed the tiny bundle of nerves until she was moving her hips up and down so fast he thought she'd jostle herself right off him.

"Come on, baby. Come for me."

She threw back her head and screamed her release, her body convulsing around his. With a firm grip on her bottom, Baldwin suddenly stood and stepped over to her desk. He lay her back on the wooden surface and began pounding into her pussy with all the abandon he'd been storing up inside.

Kena wrapped her legs around his waist and threw her arms back, holding on to the edge of the desk. "Fuck me, fuck me, fuck me," she chanted.

"Take me, take all of me." He gripped her buttocks hard and pushed her legs up over his shoulders, pistoning in long strokes and almost pulling out before impaling her again and again. The desk was shaking he was fucking her so hard. He could feel her second orgasm start to build and watched as her face contorted with pleasure.

"Ohhhh…" she gasped, crying out as the wave overtook her. Her inner walls convulsed around him, gripping at him as he fucked her. Unable to hold out much longer he thrust once, twice, and then exploded.

He collapsed, pressing his hips against hers and feeling the walls of her pussy still gripping him. Finally their breathing became smoother and he rose up and looked into her eyes.

"Tell me." Kena's eyes were glazed and unfocused, but he needed to hear her say the words. "Tell me."

"Yes, yes, it was good. More than good, it was great."

Chapter Seven

As she sat on the floor in Baldwin's office, Kena felt overwhelmed by the project ahead of her. The number of boxes strewn around the room was astronomical. There seemed to be no rhyme or reason to any of it. In the current box alone she'd found amongst other things, a high school yearbook from his sophomore year, a ticket stub to a local baseball game from two years ago, and a paper he'd written in college about quasars. The man was eclectic to say the least.

The problem was she'd discovered herself spending way too much time looking through his stuff, trying to get to know more about the man she'd started sleeping with. Although they were great together in bed, which she had so humbly admitted after their blowout sex session in her office, she still knew almost nothing about him.

The one tidbit she'd uncovered was they were both only children, about the only thing they seemed to have in common. Otherwise, it was as if they'd grown up on completely divergent paths. He'd been right about one thing, if his mother hadn't hired her, she would have never met him. He had gone to the town's other high school and then away for college.

After college he'd joined the military and lived wherever he'd been stationed. If he hadn't been injured, she didn't think he would have ever moved back home. She wasn't really sure why she believed it, but there was nothing in these boxes that told her he was tied to this town or his family. In fact, it seemed as if he'd gotten away from them as soon as he possibly could, not that she could blame him after meeting his mother.

Standing up she grabbed the yearbook, intent on getting it on the shelf so it would look like she had accomplished something. As she walked across the room she tried weaving her way through the boxes. Unfortunately, she'd never been particularly graceful. She tripped, losing her balance, and fell to her knees, dropping the annual in the process. A photograph enfolded in a slip of paper fell from the book and fluttered to the floor.

She sat back on her heels and picked up the photo and paper, wondering if it was from an old girlfriend. Instead she found it was an older picture of four young guys and a letter dated just four years ago. Even though she knew it was wrong, she began to read the letter.

Hey, Baldie!

Ha ha! Just kidding. Well, I'm off to Balad in Iraq in four days. It's my first deployment to an arena of engagement. Of course, Mom's freaking out. I should probably be scared to death, too, but you know me...I figure I'll be able to deal with whatever comes around.

Who would have thought all the old gang would end up in the military? You and me in the Air Force, Rich in the Army, Mikey in the Marines -- with all the mischief we caused in high school, I know most folks probably thought we'd never amount to much. I actually thought it might be too tough a road, at first. At least, for me. You know, since I'm used to being the one in control (wink).

I can take orders for a good cause, though. I'm gonna keep those aircraft running for our guys. I'll be with the 332nd Expeditionary Maintenance Group, working on the F-16 Fighting Falcon, MQ-1 Predator, C-130's, and the HH-60 Pave Hawks. Those days we spent rebuilding engines in Cranston's old shed have paid off for me.

Gotta go. Try to keep in touch, old buddy. And stay out of the line of fire...

Adam

She was intrigued to say the least. Although she knew Baldwin had been injured in the war, reading his friend's letter somehow made it all the more real to her. Knowing he had friends, people who cared about him, was mind boggling. He was so closemouthed she would have never guessed.

To find out he helped rebuild engines in high school was unbelievable. She never would have pegged him as the grease monkey type. There were certainly multiple layers to him.

"It doesn't look like you've gotten too far."

Poking her head up, she saw Baldwin standing in the office doorway, gazing over the sea of boxes. Before she'd started they had all been piled neatly on top of one another. She realized she now had them spread far and wide.

Smiling sheepishly, she struggled to stand. "Looks can be deceiving. I'm getting a lot organized here."

"Uh huh. It looks like a mess."

"There's good stuff here." Waving the letter at him. "I even discovered you have friends."

His face clouded over. "What the hell. Who told you to snoop through my stuff?"

She stared at him incredulously. "I believe it was you when you begged me to come back and help you organize this shit." She had refused to work for him after his mother fired her, but when he'd ask her to help him with his office she'd agreed as another way to be able to continue to have contact with him.

"I didn't beg you."

"Whatever. You wanted me to help and I did because I like you and I want to spend time with you. When I found the letter, I thought it almost made you sound human. My bad."

Kena couldn't believe he could still be such an ass. It made her wonder if he was worth the effort. Damn him for being so good in bed, because otherwise she might just be out of here already.

"Look, I'm just not used to people butting into my business."

Hands on her hips, she stared him down. "You realize I don't work for you, right? I don't have to stick around here and be yelled at. After two fucks we're practically seeing each other, but if you don't watch your attitude you may never see fuck number three."

Stepping forward, he reached out as if to grab her and then dropped his hands. "I haven't talked about my friends in a long time. I don't open up easily."

"No kidding."

Baldwin sighed heavily and dropped into the nearby leather recliner. "Adam, Rich, and Mikey were guys I met in high school."

Would wonders never cease? She was shocked and amazed at the sudden turn of events. Who was she to complain? He was actually talking, about himself no less. But instead of saying anything, she cleared off another chair across from him and sat, letting him continue.

"They were regular guys, not the country club losers my parents wanted me to hang with."

"I bet that went over well."

Baldwin shrugged his shoulders ruefully. "You've met my mother; what do you think?"

"So your nickname is Baldie??"

"Not really. It was only Adam who ever called me that. In high school I wore my hair long, so when I joined the air force and had my hair crew cut, he thought it hilarious to make a play on my name and call me Baldie."

"I can't imagine you wearing your hair long."

He smiled and shook his head. "I did just about everything in my power to rebel against my parents. I wore my hair long, made friends with the wrong kind of people, you know the usual stuff kids do."

That explained his attraction to her. "Why do I think it's more than that?"

"What do you mean?"

"If you were only doing it to rebel against your parents, why would you stay in contact with these guys all this time?"

"I haven't stayed in contact. Not really. In fact that letter was the last communication I had with any of them."

"The letter makes it sound like you were all close. What happened?"

Baldwin ran his fingers through his hair. "I don't know. I changed. I became someone I didn't like very much. How could I face my friends after that?"

Kena stared at him dubiously. "Changed how exactly?"

"I know it's probably hard for you to believe, but I was actually a fun loving guy before the war. When I got over there and saw what it was like, I don't know; it just wasn't what I expected."

"Did you think it was going to be all roses and sunshine?"

He shook his head. "No, I'm not that naïve. However, I didn't expect to be questioning why I was there."

"Did you think your friends wouldn't accept that you might not be thrilled with the whole war idea?" She knew men in the military could be a gung ho kind of bunch.

"No, it wasn't that. I knew they would understand. We're all in the military and we all know it isn't close to perfect. But after I was injured my parents offered to get me into the best rehabilitation hospital in the country. I had top-notch doctors and got the finest care available."

"Okay, it's obvious you see your parents' help as a bad thing, although why, I have no idea. I still don't understand how that destroyed your friendships."

"I never wanted to rely on my parents or their money. It's why I rebelled. I used some money I got from my grandpop to go to college, joined ROTC, and then started in the air force right after graduation. My friends knew and understood my reluctance to take anything from my parents and they supported me. Then I caved when the going was rough. I hate myself for it."

"And you think they'll hate you too?"

"I don't know."

"Would you judge them, if they did something out of the ordinary? Would you immediately cut them off without explanation?"

"No, of course not."

"Then why would you assume they would do the same thing to you?"

A look of clarity crossed his face, as he seemed to realize the truth to her words. "How is it you can hold a mirror up to my life and show me what I can't see myself?"

Kena smiled. "It's a talent. Too bad I can't do it more for myself. But hey, I have no problem showing others the errors of their ways."

Baldwin was amazed by Kena. Her presence seemed to rile him up and get him crazy, but she was also so open in her feelings he found himself telling her things he could barely admit to himself. After she'd refused to work for him but then agreed to come back to help him organize his office, he knew he wasn't willing to let her go. Somehow he knew he needed to keep her in his life.

Although he couldn't explain it, her presence made him happy. Happy to be alive, happy to have someone to argue with, happy to forget, even for a few moments, the horrors of a war he'd never wanted to be involved in. He kept wondering just how far he could push her but each time, instead of running, she pushed back. She was no weak little social butterfly, but a strong independent woman, just the kind he'd always hoped to find, but never had.

"You've got me at a disadvantage. I've spilled my guts, but I know nothing about you."

"Please, I'm an open book. What do you want to know?"

"Tell me about your family."

"My parents divorced when I was a baby and I've never been close to my dad. My mom raised me until she died when I was sixteen, then I went to live with my aunt Donna."

She stated the particulars of her life matter-of-factly, but he got the feeling the loss of her mother was much more important to her than she was admitting.

"That must have been hard, losing your mom."

Kena shrugged her shoulders. "My aunt was like a surrogate mother. She's my family, my confidante, my best friend."

"It's amazing to me how close you are with your aunt."

She chuckled. "With your family I'm not surprised. It's like you're a changeling."

"That's a word for it. The sad thing is they're not bad people, just a bit...misdirected. My mother's family didn't have money until she was in high school, so I think she's always trying to prove to everyone she belongs in the social club circle."

"You don't talk much about your dad. What's he like?"

Baldwin watched Kena swing her foot as she spoke and reached out to grab hold of her ankle the next time she swung out. Instead of pulling back, as he had thought she might, she cocked her eyebrow, but said nothing. Placing her foot in his lap, he began to untie the laces on her shoe as he answered her.

"My father's quiet and, unfortunately, a bit controlled by my mother. Instead of standing up to her, he became this workaholic I never really knew. It's sad to say, but he wasn't someone I wanted to emulate. My grandpop, who left me this house, was the biggest influence in my life next to my friends."

While he spoke he removed her shoe and began massaging her foot. He watched as a content look came over her face.

"Have you ever thought about contacting them?"

His hand paused in his ministrations to her foot, but she nudged at him to continue. "For what purpose?"

She released a heavy sigh before answering. "Because you just said that besides your grandfather, they were the most influential people in your life. Wouldn't you want to see how they're doing now, know if they're married or even alive?"

"I never thought about it before." And he hadn't. Instead he'd dismissed the men, figuring he didn't deserve their friendship. But Kena's words once again had him wondering if he'd ever truly thought about it at all or had just made certain assumptions based on his own feelings. Adam, Rich, and Mikey were the best friends he'd ever had. Maybe he should try to contact them.

Before he could continue that line of thought, however, he became distracted by Kena's foot in his lap. While he'd been ruminating he'd stopped massaging and so she'd taken to doing some exploring of her own. Her toes had run over the ridge of his now growing erection, teasing him to semi-hardness.

Looking into her eyes he knew she understood exactly what she had been doing. As he sat and brooded, she had decided to play. Somehow she always seemed to know what he needed. He grabbed her foot, holding her fast.

"Little girls who tease get punished."

Kena smiled seductively, biting her bottom lip. "Sounds interesting. Punished how?"

"It's no fun if you know ahead of time. Besides, it's punishment. You're not supposed to be looking forward to it."

"Hmm, I see." She started to unbutton her blouse, slowly revealing tempting glimpses of her mocha skin. He could feel his body reacting to her obvious interest. "Have you always had this kinky side to your personality?"

"Kinky?"

"Yeah." She waggled her eyebrows suggestively. "Maybe I could dig up my old high school uniform. Would you like to give me my punishment while I wear it?"

He knew she was teasing, but the idea wasn't without merit. In fact, he could just imagine flipping up her plaid skirt to reveal her panty-clad ass. He'd pull down the white cotton underwear to reveal her curves. That scenario definitely had some possibilities.

"Hey, I don't think I like that look in your eyes." She'd pulled her foot from his grasp and was sitting poised on her chair as if to escape.

"Don't offer something you're not prepared to follow through on."

"See, I told you. Kinky." She looked torn between laughter and yearning.

"Maybe I am."

"I don't have my school uniform here."

"Too bad, but I bet we could find something else to do." His mind was awash with all the thoughts she'd suddenly put there. He'd always been a dominant lover, but he'd never tried bondage. The thought of tying her down and having her at his mercy held some appeal. In fact, it was downright arousing.

Her eyes shifted back and forth and he knew the moment she was going to run. She jumped up from the chair and he let her slip by him, although he could have easily stopped her flight right there. Instead, he stood and followed as she sprinted out the door.

Rather than head downstairs, she'd run down the hallway and into his bedroom. Baldwin was shocked at the pleasure he felt coursing through his body. Deliberate in his movements he headed toward his destination. Reaching the doorway of his room, he actually smiled at the sight before his eyes.

Kena was standing at the foot of the bed, legs spread slightly and arms braced on the mattress. What should have surprised him, but didn't, was how she had pulled her shorts down to mid thigh, baring her ass to his lust-filled gaze. The reality was much better than the image in his head had been. Walking forward, he palmed her bottom, squeezing the firm flesh.

She moaned and wiggled her ass in invitation. Standing back he spanked her right cheek, watching as she jerked slightly at the impact. He landed three more blows in quick succession, alternating on each side. Although the smacks must have been a shock, she didn't flinch from his touch. In fact, if he wasn't mistaken, he was pretty sure she was becoming excited. He was sure he could smell her unique musk permeating the air.

Dipping his fingers between her legs he found her wet with arousal. She pushed back against him as he explored her soft cleft.

"I guess it's too late to remind you you're not supposed to enjoy the punishment."

Turning her head, she licked her lips before answering. "I guess you'll have to think of another punishment."

Baldwin smiled wickedly, knowing just what he had in mind.

Chapter Eight

Kena shivered when Baldwin stepped away from her for a moment. Her ass was fiery hot from the spanking she'd received, but her pussy was damn near drowning from excitement. Finding a lover who liked to play during sex was a bonus, in her opinion. It was something she always hoped for, but it rarely ever happened.

Whipping her head around, she realized he was no longer in the room. Now she was beginning to wonder why she was still bent over the bed with her ass in the air. As she started to straighten, however, his hand smacked across her rear, effectively halting her movements.

"Hey!" She desperately wanted to rub the aching flesh, but he took over that task, massaging the ache he had administered.

"Hey what? I step away for one minute and already you're done?"

"I thought you left."

"Just for that, more punishment. And, to make it a bit more interesting, how about we try this?" Before she had a chance to comprehend what he was talking about, a silk cloth was placed over her eyes, blocking her vision.

The loss of her eyesight had her other senses on overdrive. She strained to track his movements as she heard him opening and closing drawers before returning to her side.

"Climb up on the bed."

She debated for a moment and then brazenly shimmied out of her shorts and panties. Due to her sightless state, Baldwin graciously helped her up on the bed. She felt a bit ridiculous, sitting there with a blindfold over her eyes, her bra on and blouse gaping open, but completely nude otherwise. On the other hand, she was sure she wouldn't be wearing the other garments much longer.

"Now what?" She realized she sounded a bit nervous when instead of her usual firm tone her voice was husky and broken.

"As sexy as they look, why don't you lose the bra and blouse and then lay back for me."

Stripping off the rest of her clothing, Kena did as he instructed. The touch of his hand along her arm had her shivering and not from the cold. She felt something wrap around her wrist and realized he'd secured her to the bed. Her other wrist received the same treatment and she soon found her arms spread wide over her head.

"I'll be right back." He ran his hand down the length of her body as he made that statement and then he left the room. She lay bound to his bed, wondering just what the hell he was doing. Surprisingly, she wasn't scared to be left like this, only thoughtful in anticipation of what was to come. Thankfully she didn't have to wait too long as she heard him return and set something on the bedside table before joining her on the bed.

She felt a drip of cool water on her lips, moments before it was licked away by his tongue. It must have come from an ice cube, because the next thing she felt was it painting her lips before traveling down her chin to rub along her neck. She whooped with surprise.

"That's freaking cold."

Baldwin chuckled at her reaction as he traced the delicate lines of her collarbone before dipping between her breasts and traveling downward to circle her belly button. Although he really wasn't touching her in any sexual way, she was practically squirming on the bed, hoping he would. Finally beginning to adapt to the cold torture, she was more aware than ever of her body's reaction to his teasing touch.

She gasped as he blew across her stomach before lazily coating her breast in ever smaller concentric circles. Her nipple was puckered in anticipation of the frozen touch, but instead he left it untreated and moved to the other breast, leaving her panting in anticipation. By the time he finished with her second breast, she was straining with need.

"Touch me."

"I am touching you."

"No, damn you. Touch my nipples."

"Like this?" He brushed the back of his hand lightly across the tips of her breasts, barely making contact.

"Please don't tease me." Kena wasn't above begging at this point, if that was what it took.

"No, I don't think so. I like teasing you."

She whimpered at the thought of how he could torture her, but comforted herself with the thought he'd give in eventually. Unfortunately, she didn't anticipate how much of an iron will he'd have. Baldwin proceeded to move down her body, covering the entire length with melting cubes. By the time he was done, Kena was shivering from the need to have him touch her aching breasts and pussy.

"Please, Baldwin, I can't stand it."

Without warning he touched the tip of her breast with the ice, rubbing her taut nipple until she thought she'd scream with the pleasure. But Kena had no idea what was in store, because as he moved the ice cube to her other nipple, his mouth enclosed the dripping wet nub he'd just coated.

His tongue licked and teased at her nipple, his warm mouth a stark contrast to the cool flesh. She pulled at her restraints, now wishing she was free so she could hold on to something. He suddenly released her with a pop and turned to tease her other breast. His hand still held that maddening cube of ice and he wasn't done using it yet.

As he continued his attention to her breasts, he reached for something and then cupped his hand between her thighs. With a fresh piece of ice in his hand, she jumped at his first touch on her sensitive pussy. Rubbing it along her lips, Baldwin reversed direction and pressed the ice against her swollen clit.

"Shit, that's cold." Although her voice was complaining, her hips were raised, pressing hard against his hand. He continued to rub the ice along her pussy and the insides of her thigh, thoroughly coating her with the melting water.

Finally releasing her nipple, he sat up for a moment. The ice cube he'd been torturing her with had faded away, but he still had a few tricks up his sleeve. When he pushed a finger inside her, she moaned and arched her back, craving his deeper penetration. His thumb began circling her clit as he continued to thrust deep, gradually adding a second and then third finger.

He kissed down her body, licking lightly at her breasts before moving down her stomach toward his plunging fingers. Her muscles were gripping him hard, trying to hold him inside her. His digits and wickedly circling thumb were pushing her to the limits. But when he moved his thumb away from her clit and swiped his tongue across the sensitive bundle of flesh, she thought she might just explode right then and there.

"Ohmygod, ohmygod." She held on tightly to the material binding her to the bed as she dug her feet into the mattress and arched her hips toward him, desperately aching for more of his mouth on her.

As he pulled his fingers out of her body, she cried out in despair. But he didn't keep her empty for long, sliding his tongue inside and stabbing into her depths.

"No more, I can't stand it."

The bastard chuckled at her response, laughing at her need. He blew across her clit, his warm breath tickling her sensitive flesh. Then, pushing his fingers deep inside once again, he leaned down to suck her clit into his mouth, biting gently, and driving her over the edge into climax.

"Baldwin, Baldwin, Baldwin." She chanted his name as she came. Although she lay in a daze from her mind-shattering orgasm, she was far from ready for their playtime to be over.

"Do I get to return the favor?"

He swept his hand over her stomach, causing an additional shiver to race through her body.

"What, tie me to the bed and have your wicked way with me?"

"Hmm, that sounds nice, but no, we don't have to go that far. How about I just drive you to distraction with my mouth until you're a pool of jelly? All you have to do is untie me."

His low chuckle had her clenching with need. "As good as that sounds, I think I like having you at my mercy."

She shivered in anticipation at the pleasures to come promised in his deep resonating voice.

He stepped away from the bed for a moment, watching as she turned her head toward his every movement. He quickly stripped off his shirt then toed off his shoes before pushing his jeans and briefs down over his hips to pool on the floor. Kneeling on the bed next to her head, he took his erection in hand.

"Although I'm not ready to untie you, your suggestion sounded pretty interesting."

He watched as she smiled seductively before parting her lips, inviting him to enter. Moving forward, he fed his cock into her mouth. When she made contact with him, she leaned up and licked at the tip, delicately at first, but then with firmer strokes. He moaned in encouragement and she opened her mouth, sucking the tip and swirling her tongue around the crown.

"That's so good."

Kena released him for a moment and he moved to straddle her body so he was now in front of her. She opened her mouth again and started licking along his length. He reached out and touched her hair, grasping the silken strands in his hands.

"Come on, baby, suck me, swallow it."

She began to suck on him, shifting her lips back and forth as she took him deeper and deeper into her throat. He was now moving in rhythm to her motions, rocking his hips forward with her every advance. The sensations were rocketing through him and as enticing as it was to come in her mouth, he still wanted to fuck her.

"Kena, baby, I'm going to come."

Baldwin tried to pull back from her, but she surprised him by trying to follow as he retreated. Only her restraints stopped her progress and he was finally able to move away from her delectable mouth.

"I wanted you to come in my mouth." She pouted.

He chuckled at her sulkiness. "No, I want to fuck you."

He watched her body react to his words. She looked beautiful lying bound before him, stretched out as if a sacrifice for his pleasure. His cock was rock hard and he wanted to plunge into her heated depths, but he also wanted to make this moment last.

He leaned down and angled his head to capture her mouth. Kena met his ferocity with eagerness, tangling her tongue with his. Her legs shifted restlessly beneath him and he briefly thought about securing them as well, but he didn't have anything else he could use to tie her down. Breaking their kiss, he leaned back and watched as she tried to catch her breath.

"I want to touch you." She tugged again at her restraints.

"Later."

Before things spiraled out of control, he opened his bedside table and pulled out a foil-wrapped condom. Ripping it open, he quickly rolled it over his erection. Then reaching down between them, Baldwin bent her legs and pushed them open wide, exposing her to his gaze.

"God, you're beautiful." His fingers combed through the dark curls covering her treasures.

She whimpered. "Please…"

"Do you want me?"

"Yes." Her answer came in a rush, as if she were afraid he would change his mind.

"Then ask me."

Without hesitation she whispered, "Fuck me, Baldwin."

Kneeling before her, he parted her nether lips with the head of his cock. Instead of immediately thrusting inside, he coated himself with her essence, moving the head around her lips, up to her clit, slow and teasing. He eventually pushed himself into her, pulling back out and pushing in again and again, teasing her with his every movement.

"Damn it, stop teasing and fuck me."

He plunged into her deep and quick, answering her plea, before once again drawing back.

"Baldwin…" she wailed, tugging at her bindings.

He began thrusting again, slowly, each time a little deeper. His hands held her ass cheeks, keeping her still as he propelled himself forward. Every inch of his hard cock was going into her, his sac slapping her ass with every movement. He pulled back slower than he went in, and drove deeper.

"Tell me again."

"Fuck meeee --" Her voice caught as he thrust forward before again drawing back, almost slipping free of the warm clasp of her body.

"Demanding aren't you?"

"Please, don't make me beg."

Beg. Although the idea was tempting, he hadn't just been teasing her, but himself as well. Unable to resist any longer, he pushed back inside. He began to move harder and faster, and his breathing became heavier. His cock filled her pussy with every movement, taking him all in, deeper with each driving force.

His balls slapped against her as he moved faster and faster. Her moaning was louder and she wrapped her legs around his waist. She was ready to come and she clamped down on his cock, squeezing him in her silken clasp.

She let out a scream as she exploded with the intensity of her orgasm. Her pussy quivered uncontrollably and he could barely hold back his own climax. Pulling from her warmth he reached down between them and stroked her, gathering the dew there.

"Mmm, that's nice." She moaned her appreciation and tipped her hips forward in encouragement.

Her legs started to quiver as he took his middle finger, now coated in her juices, and began to tease her rosette.

"Uh, what are you doing?"

"You know what I'm doing."

He watched as she held her breath while he slowly started to push into her ass. He could feel the tightness slowly give way as he slid in past the first knuckle then eventually the second.

"Oooo, I don't know about this."

"Just relax and we'll go slowly."

She released a quivering sigh as he started to move his finger in and out of her rear. Although she didn't say anything, he could tell this was a brand-new experience for her. Slowly the pressure on his probing digit started to lessen and he was able to move more freely.

"Do you like this?" he asked as he continued to play with her bottom.

"Oh, God yes. I never thought…" Suddenly she gasped as he curled his finger up inside her, stroking against her internally.

Adjusting his position on the bed, he brought his other hand into play, sliding a digit into her pussy and stroking his thumb over her clit.

"Oooo, yes." Kena was thrashing her head back and forth as he fucked both her holes at the same time. He knew she could feel them rubbing together through the thin membrane inside of her.

Again her hips started to buck under the pressure of his manipulations, her own movements pushing them deeper and deeper inside her. She cried out when she came, her juices flowing out over his hand as both her pussy and her ass clenched hard at his fingers inside her.

As she came down from her climax he leaned forward, kissing along her jawline. "I want to fuck you here." He wiggled the digit in her rear and her body shivered in response to his words.

"Yes, fuck me, fuck my ass, please." She was pushing back against him.

He pulled his finger from her body. As he knelt between her spread open thighs, she was totally exposed to him. He quickly lubed his condom-covered erection as well as her rosette before positioning his cock at her entrance. Draping her legs over his shoulders he slowly pressed forward.

"You're a lot bigger than a finger." She panted as he inched ahead.

He paused for a minute. "Same rules apply, just relax and we'll take it slow."

Kena's breath came out in harsh gasps as he carefully pushed inside her ass.

"I feel so full."

When he was finally lodged balls deep, he stopped for a minute to stare down at her. Her arms were still spread wide and her eyes were covered. The legs he'd thrown over his shoulders were now locked around him. Reaching out he brushed her sweat-soaked hair away from her forehead.

"You doing okay, baby?"

She nodded, but he wanted to make sure.

"No, talk to me."

"I'm good; it's just…so different, but good."

He pulled back and began fucking her, a nice slow rhythm. He watched and waited and she soon began to relax, joining him in the rocking motions. Little by little he began to move faster, pulling almost fully out before slamming back into her. She was thrusting back against him, squeezing her internal muscles as he fucked her.

"Oh God, fuck me, harder, harder."

Supporting himself with one hand he reached between them and found her clit. He started frigging it and she bucked against his hand, drawing his cock even farther into her ass.

"Oh fuck, I'm going to come," she cried as she thrashed about. She began to convulse around him. He gasped and plunged forward, driving her back down into the mattress. His cock swelled even larger, digging deeper than ever, and then began to pulse inside her.

Baldwin collapsed on her prostrate body, unable to move for a few moments. He then pulled away from her and rolled over onto his back, trying to regain his breath. Finally standing, he disposed of the condom in the bathroom and then returned to the bed.

Kena laid still, her arms hanging loosely above her. Quickly untying her from her restraints, he gently massaged her arms.

"You're going to bruise from all that pulling."

She lifted her hand to push the blindfold off her eyes and blinked at the brightness of the room. "I don't mind if you don't."

"I wish I could pick you up and carry you into the bathroom, but...I can run a nice bubble bath for you."

Smiling, she stood and pulled him up to stand beside her. "Are you going to join me? I know that tub is big enough for two."

"I'd be happy to wash your back."

Chapter Nine

It had been three days since Kena had seen Baldwin and she was missing him terribly. They'd spent a sex-filled weekend together, but by Sunday night she knew she needed some space to evaluate what was going on. Instead of examining her feelings for him, however, she'd thrown herself into work and skillfully avoiding his calls.

If it had just been a sexual connection, she could push it off as some kind of hard up infatuation. Hell, it's not as if she'd been seeing anyone since starting her business. Kena could just tell herself she was in need of some cock and write it off as hot sex and nothing more.

But they'd talked, and she'd found they had more in common than she'd initially realized. They enjoyed the same music, the same foods; they even had the same sense of humor when it came to cult classic movies. There was just one niggling worry that continued to plague Kena. She wondered why he refused to talk about his issues about being injured. She had a feeling there was something else there, just under the surface, but it was the one thing he hadn't readily opened up about.

When her phone rang, she glanced at the caller identification and saw that it was Baldwin calling again. Instead of letting it go to voice mail she decided to answer.

"Hello." The silence at the other end had her wondering for a moment if she'd cut him off. "Hello?"

"Yeah, I'm here. Sorry, I just didn't expect you to answer."

Guilt was a very effective tool when used on a person who had every right to feel guilty.

"I've been pretty busy the last few days. How have you been?"

"We're really not going to do the small talk thing, are we?"

Um, guess not. "Okay, let's cut to the chase then."

"I want to take you out to dinner."

Of all the things she thought he might say, that wasn't one of them. Perhaps instead of avoiding him she should try spending time with him outside the bedroom.

"I'd love to."

Another long pause. "Good, I'll pick you up at seven o'clock."

Glancing at her watch, she realized that only gave her an hour to get ready so she quickly ended the call. She raced through her shower and makeup and then spent the rest of the time deciding what to wear. Since she hadn't bothered to find out where they were going, she went middle of the road and wore a floral print skirt and red blouse.

She was showered, dressed, made-up, and ready to go with five minutes to spare, which she then spent pacing the living room, to the delight of her aunt.

"I've never seen you so gone over a man before. This guy must be something special."

"We'll see." Kena wasn't ready to make any commitments yet. She was still too worried about getting her heart broken.

When the doorbell rang precisely at seven o'clock, she jumped up to answer. Baldwin was dressed in a similar casual fashion with khaki pants, blue shirt, and suede jacket.

He smiled when he saw her standing there. "You look beautiful." Pulling her into his arms he kissed her soundly, chasing thoughts of their audience from her head until the clearing throat finally caught her attention and she broke their embrace.

"Thank you." Turning, she pulled him into the room. "I'd like to introduce you to my aunt Donna."

Her aunt shook his hand and asked a few pointed questions while at the same time giving her their special sign for "this looks like a good one." After a good five-minute interrogation, Kena was finally able to pull him away from her aunt and they headed toward the car. He held the door open for her and then walked around to the driver's side. He slipped behind the wheel and they were soon on their way to the restaurant.

"I didn't realize I'd be getting the third degree."

"Come on, you should have at least expected the 'what are your intentions' question."

"I suppose so. After all, I did hold you captive all weekend."

"A willing one."

He turned to give her a speculative look, but didn't comment. They chatted about inconsequential things during the rest of the ride and before long they reached the restaurant. He'd made reservations so they didn't wait long to be seated at their table. There was even a bottle of wine waiting chilled at the table. She felt as if an evening of seduction had begun.

"This is a really nice place. I've wanted to check it out." Truthfully, she always thought her bank account wouldn't allow her to spend the kind of money it took to eat at a place like this. But after reviewing the menu she discovered it wasn't quite as expensive as she'd feared. And looking around the room, she noticed the patrons weren't all dressed in cocktail dresses and suits as she'd imagined they would be.

"I'm glad you approve."

"I do, it's --" She trailed off as applause broke out for a couple entering the restaurant both dressed in military uniform. Some people even stood to shake their hands. As she turned back to Baldwin she noted a look of dismay on his face before he quickly masked it. "So you were in the air force, right?"

"Yes."

So much for that opening gambit. Their waiter arrived and they ordered dinner. Jumping right back into the fray, she said, "I bet you never tire of seeing stuff like that."

"Like what?"

"You know, the applause, the appreciation for a job well done."

"Not everyone deserves that kind of esteem."

That comment set her back for a moment. "You don't think the soldiers merit our admiration?"

"I was referring to myself."

Whoa, that wasn't what she'd been expecting at all. "I'm confused. Why don't you think you deserve that kind of respect?"

Baldwin ran his hands over his face wearily. "I don't think this is the place to be having this conversation."

"Well then, where is the place? Because it's not like you've ever brought it up before. Do you only have these kinds of conversations somewhere special I've never heard of?"

"What I should have said is I don't want to be having this conversation, here or anywhere else."

Kena knew he thought he'd effectively shut her down with that statement, but what he'd actually done was ignite her ire. "I'm sorry, but you made the statement. It's out there. I'm not going to let it go, so why don't you just explain to me why everyone else deserves kudos except for you."

"Why can't you just respect the fact I don't want to talk about this and let's enjoy a nice dinner?"

She weighed the options in her mind. He had a point. If he didn't want to talk about it, why was she so insistent on pushing him? Perhaps it was just her own insecurities about their burgeoning relationship that made her want him to open up to her.

"I'm sorry; I'm just one of those people who speaks her mind, which includes asking uncomfortable questions. If you really don't want to tell me then don't."

"You wouldn't understand."

"Then make me understand, explain it to me."

Baldwin sighed heavily, looking like he was going to his execution. "Fine, you want to know why I don't deserve appreciation for a job well done? I deserted the soldiers in my unit. There, are you happy, satisfied now that you've discovered my deep, dark secret?" His words were laced heavily with sarcasm as he spit out the last line.

Kena might not know everything about Baldwin, but she just didn't see him as a coward. There had to be more to this story than he was revealing.

"Why don't you tell me the real story instead of hiding behind this fake martyrdom?"

He shook his head incredulously. "I don't care what you think you know or don't know. You've never served and you can't understand what it's like to be living with strangers day in and day out. They become your family, more than your own blood relations in a way, because you're relying on them for your life every single day."

He never raised his voice, but his tone was coldly furious. If she was smart she'd shut up, but she'd never pretended to take the easy way out. And since she had already pushed this far, she might as well go for broke.

"I don't buy that argument. I understand plenty of things I don't have personal experience with. You're a pretty smart man, I think if you really wanted to you could make me understand. Use small words."

He stared at her with disbelief, unable to comprehend her brazenness. How dare she presume to judge him?

"Are you deliberately this antagonistic to everyone you meet?"

"No, only to those people I'm close to. And don't think you can change the subject that easily."

She was like a dog with a bone and not likely to give up any time soon. Unfortunately, remembering the incident that led to his surgery usually put him in a pensive mood.

"My unit was part of an escort group for civilian contractors. We were just outside of Baghdad when we were hit by a sniper. It caused a chain reaction accident that left most of my unit and the group of contractors injured."

He found it kind of interesting that she had now seemingly decided to remain quiet while he told his story. Picking up his wine, he took a swallow before continuing.

"I was one of the lucky ones. My vehicle wasn't hit, so all of my injuries were sustained from shrapnel from another truck that exploded. Some of the guys weren't so lucky. They died that day."

"I'm so sorry." She looked as if she wanted to say more, but he knew how she felt and nodded in understanding. What could be said about something so senseless? They had died driving around in the desert, doing what would be a normal everyday job at any other time and place.

Seemingly without thought he reached across the table and took her hand in his. "Most of the injured in my unit were transferred to Germany and then back here to the States for treatment at the VA hospital. I can't even describe to you what a horrible place it was. No one would ever want to be there."

"It must have been awful for you."

He grimaced in remembrance of the sights, smells, and noises he knew time would never erase from his memory. The recollections from his actual injury were few because he'd been unconscious, but the hospital he remembered only too well.

"It was awful for everyone. When my parents arrived and said they'd secured admission for me into a private rehabilitation hospital, I jumped at the chance."

"Of course you would." She stroked his hand in comfort and he wondered how long it would be before she drew back in distaste when she understood the truth.

"You don't understand. I had forsaken them and everything they stood for since I turned eighteen. I had sworn I would never use money like they did. But as soon as I had the chance, I threw all my convictions to the wind."

At the time they'd made the offer he hadn't blinked an eye and had immediately jumped at the chance to leave. As soon as they received the word, he'd been moved to the new location in a matter of days. It was only after he'd arrived that he began to experience the pangs of guilt and sporadic nightmares.

"Just because you took advantage of a gift given to you by your parents, doesn't make you a bad person. You did nothing wrong."

"How can you say that? I left the hellhole and went to a hospital that looked like a spa and where I was treated as if I were royalty. All the while leaving my unit to suffer on in squalor."

"I think you're beating yourself up for no reason. Don't you think any one of them would have traded places with you in an instant?"

"They didn't have the opportunity."

She rolled her eyes dramatically. "So what, you think it would have been better to stay in squalor with them? Give me a break. Any doctor would have had you committed if you made such a stupid choice. And the members of your unit would have thought you were an idiot just to stay on principle."

"Maybe so. But every day I think about those who had to stay behind and wonder why me."

He questioned daily what had happened to many of the men and women he'd known, but never visited, not wanting to see the way he'd left them. He'd even begun calling the VA hospital to try and get updates on the members of his unit but due to the privacy laws they wouldn't release any information.

"That's like asking yourself why you were only injured when others died in the attack. It wasn't your time. It's the luck of the draw."

"No, it's not the same thing. In the hospital the only difference between me and the thousands others there was my parents' wealth."

"So boohoo, they have money and they used it to help their son. Sorry, I may not be a fan of your mother's but I'm on her side on this one. I'd do anything and everything for my kid, damn the consequences."

"I'm not blaming my parents. I just don't think I deserve applause and accolades."

As he spoke the words though, he realized it wasn't true. He did blame them in a way. He took the opportunity his parents gave him while pushing them away when they tried to get close. It was as if he no longer wanted to be associated with what their presence represented.

"I'm sorry, but I have to disagree with you. You served your country and were injured in the process. You made choices any reasonable person would have made. You survived and if nothing else you should be proud of it. If taking advantage of your parents' wealth really bothers you so much, then do something about it. But don't keep feeling sorry for yourself or trying to hide behind the guilt. It's not getting you anywhere."

Baldwin contemplated her words. He'd never shared his entire story with anyone, not his family or the doctors, believing people would condemn his choices. But judging from Kena's reactions, she wasn't as concerned about him leaving the hospital as she was about how he'd been acting since then.

When their waiter arrived with their food, he was surprised to realize how little time had actually passed in the telling of his story. Something that had seemed earth shattering to him was merely an infinitesimal moment in time to the rest of the world. He also suddenly recognized that it was only after their food had arrived that Kena had withdrawn her hand from his. His earlier worry that she'd be disgusted by his action hadn't come to fruition.

They spent the rest of the evening in superficial conversation. When dinner was over, he drove her home, his mind racing from one thought to another as he analyzed her perspective. Walking her to the door, he noticed she smiled at him a bit sadly.

"Am I going to get a good-night kiss at least?"

"Are you trying to tell me this hasn't been the most spectacular date you've ever been on?"

"I usually don't insult most of my dates and antagonize them, as you were so right to point out."

"Don't worry about it."

"How can't I? I might have fucked up any chance at date number two at this rate."

Baldwin stepped forward, causing her to step away in reaction, effectively placing her back against the closed front door. Although the porch light was on, it was dim and provided just the right mood lighting.

"I don't think you need to worry about a second date. I'm intrigued by women who aren't scared off by my nasty ass attitude."

He placed his hands on the door on either side of her head. His hips pressed into hers. As soon as he'd placed her in the position he watched as her eyes dilated and her breathing changed. She wanted him just as much as he wanted her, even now.

"Well it's a good thing I don't scare easily."

"A very good thing. Now about that good-night kiss."

He bent his head to capture her lips. This was no hurried contact as their tongues met each other and danced. He took his time to explore the recesses of her mouth all the while keeping the rest of his body away from hers. Soon, however, that was not enough for Kena and she reached out to slip her arms around his waist, pulling his hips toward hers.

He was easily drawn into her embrace as her pelvis cradled his growing erection. Deepening the kiss, he finally moved his hands away from the door, cupping the nape of her neck with one and grasping her hip with the other. Slowly but surely he began to pull her skirt up her legs, intent on exploring what was underneath.

Her nimble fingers began to do some exploring of their own and she'd pulled his shirt free of his trousers and slipped her hands under the material. Her touches made him want to forget everything around them and fuck her wildly against the door. Instead, he finally broke away from her mouth and leaned his head against hers as he struggled to regain his breath.

"You're not coming in, are you?" Her voice was roughened with passion.

Lifting his head he smoothed her hair from her brow and traced his finger along her cheek.

"No, I've got some thinking to do. But I want to see you again -- soon." Very, very soon. Naked preferably and bound to his bed once more. Oh yes. This was not the end of them. Only the beginning.

Chapter Ten

After their dinner date, she and Baldwin had talked on the phone almost every day, but for one reason or another, they weren't able to actually see each other. Last night, however, he had asked her if she could come over to the house the next day. He said there was something he wanted to talk to her about and it obviously wasn't something he felt comfortable talking about over the phone.

Getting ready for work the next morning she was a bundle of nerves. As she prepared breakfast she decided to ask her aunt's advice.

"Do you think I'm crazy?"

"I can't make those decisions for you, sweetie. Only you know how you feel."

"That's the problem. In some ways it feels so right, as if we're meant for each other. But then I remember we've known each other less than a month."

"Why does the time frame worry you so much?"

"You can't fall in love that quickly."

Her aunt cocked her head in thought. "Perhaps not, but you can start down the road to love."

Kena mulled over her aunt's words. She realized if she knew how Baldwin felt about their relationship she herself might not be so anxious. Instead of driving herself crazy attempting to speculate about what he wanted to share with her, she decided to try and put it out of her mind. She arrived at his house after her morning cleaning job only to find a note on the door.

Go ahead and let yourself in. I'll be back soon.

She unlocked the house and headed into the kitchen. Surprisingly, he'd been able to keep it pretty clean since she'd left. Grabbing a glass, she filled it with ice and was getting ready to pour herself some water when she heard someone walking into the kitchen.

"I've got to say you're keeping the place up."

She turned around only to stifle the scream that threatened to erupt when she saw Mrs. Garrett standing in the doorway instead of Baldwin. Unfortunately, she'd also jumped in fright and lost her grip on the glass. It hit the floor and shattered.

"Oh no." She dropped to a squat and began picking up the larger pieces of ice and glass. Standing, she dumped everything into the trash and picked up the broom and dust pan. Mrs. Garrett was still standing there, a look of disbelief on her face. They stared at each other for a minute, neither one seemingly willing to speak.

"Didn't I fire you?"

"Umm, yes you did."

"Did my son hire you?" Not giving Kena the time to answer, she bulldozed on. "I don't know what kind of sob story you gave him about needing a job, but it is highly unethical for you to be worming your way back into this position after being fired. You're obviously a menace."

"No, he didn't hire me." She didn't feel the need to explain herself to his mother.

"Did you break in?"

"Of course not."

"Then what are you doing here?"

Kena didn't want to answer her, she just wanted to leave. Damn it, how did she get stuck talking to his mother? Where the hell was he? Quickly sweeping up the remainder of the mess she decided retreating to the backyard was her best bet.

"If you'll excuse me." Kena started to make her way across the room, but as she moved past the other woman she was stopped short by her haughty words.

"I asked you a question. Why are you here?"

She wasn't in the mood to be browbeaten by this lady. His mother obviously didn't like her, but she didn't have to act so stuck up. Instead of trying to defend why she was there, Kena decided to turn the question around on the other woman.

"It's none of your business what I'm doing here. This is Baldwin's house, not yours."

"You're trespassing in my son's house. I have every right to question you. In fact, I should call the police."

"Actually, you're the one trespassing, since I was invited to be here and you just let yourself in. Besides, you seem like a smart woman. I think you can figure out exactly what I'm doing here." She raised her eyebrows expressively and watched as Baldwin's mother started to blush. Oh yeah, the woman was far from stupid.

"I just don't understand what he sees in you." His mother eyed her attire with a sniff. "You might think you've got my son wrapped around your little finger, but he'll only keep you around until the novelty wears off. He needs to find the right kind of woman, not some *housecleaner.*"

Kena wasn't really interested in getting into an argument with her, but damn, the woman could be a real bitch.

"I am not going to discuss my relationship with your son. Frankly, I doubt he will either, so why don't you give it a rest."

"Relationship? That's rich. He's sleeping with you, nothing more." She waved her hand dismissively. "I thought Gloria was the girl for him, but perhaps not. However, I'll eventually find someone who he'll be willing to settle down with and then you'll be history. So enjoy it while it lasts."

Kena could hardly believe there were mothers actually like this. "Do you hear the words you're spouting? *Someone he'll be willing to settle down with.* Shouldn't you be hoping he'll fall in love?"

"Are you suggesting you're the woman he'll fall in love with?"

"I'm not suggesting anything. I just think you should butt out."

"Why don't you mind your own advice, dear? Stick with your own kind and leave my son alone."

"My own kind?"

The woman at least had the decency to flush. Kena had pegged her as class conscious early on, but she didn't figure her for a racist as well, although she shouldn't be surprised.

"You know what I mean."

"Yes, unfortunately, I do. Thankfully, Baldwin didn't inherit your backward beliefs."

"Look, now that my son is out of the military and thankfully home he'll be looking to start a new career. He's going to need the right type of wife to do that."

"What makes you think he wanted to leave the military or is interested in any career you have in mind for him? You have no idea what Baldwin wants or needs."

"How dare you tell me about my son?"

"I dare because I care about your son. And I think you do too, so stop being so controlling and open your eyes."

"What the hell is going on here?"

Oh shit, Baldwin was home.

Looking up she saw him standing in the doorway of the kitchen, his face thunderous. She wasn't sure if he'd heard her blurt out that she cared for him, but she was pretty sure he had heard the raised voices. There was nothing like fighting with the mother of the man she was trying to build a relationship with.

"Oh, Baldwin, the woman was here when I arrived and she's been absolutely insulting." His mother immediately put on the "woe is me" act. Kena had to restrain herself from spitting out some more insults.

"She's here because I invited her to be here, Mother. Why are you here?"

"I just wanted to visit. I mean you're here all alone ever since you threw Gloria out." Mrs. Garrett turned to glare daggers at her. "Besides, I fired her so I wasn't expecting to walk in and find her prowling through your kitchen."

Kena opened her mouth to respond, but was waylaid by him raising his hand. "I wouldn't remind me you were the one who fired her, Mother."

His mother drew herself up, the stick in her ass protruding all the way through her spine. "Are you taking her side over mine?"

"There are no sides here unless you make it that way." Baldwin walked across the room to Kena, wrapping his arm around her shoulders. Although he said there were no sides he was making it abundantly clear, to her at least, that he was supporting her.

"I wanted to talk to you."

"So talk."

Mrs. Garrett stared at him pointedly. "This is a family issue, Baldwin."

She was grateful for his support, but she didn't want him to be totally alienated from his family either. Stepping away from him, she said, "Why don't I go out to the gardens for a moment while you two talk."

She quickly slipped out the back door before he could stop her.

Turning back toward his mother, Baldwin tried to control his temper. He loved her; he really did. It was only unfortunate he had to keep telling himself that.

"I'm very disappointed in you."

What was new? "Why now?"

"I never thought I would raise a son who would allow a stranger to insult his own mother."

It was time for some hard truths. "You're more a stranger to me than she is."

His mother actually took a step back, as if she'd been physically wounded by his remark. "I can't believe you said that."

"Mother, it's true. I haven't been home for more than three days since I was eighteen years old. I'm an adult now."

"I know, but you'll always be my child as well."

"Very true." This was getting them nowhere and he wasn't in the mood to argue with her. As civilly as he could, he tried again. "So what did you want to discuss?"

"I wanted to invite you for Sunday dinner. If your father and I are really strangers, perhaps we can begin to know each other again."

He strongly suspected this was just another attempt to fix him up with someone. However, maybe it was time to try and reconnect with them.

"Can I bring a guest?"

"Oh, Baldwin, I don't think…" His mother glanced from him to the backyard, her face reflecting all her dismay and doubt. Surprisingly he saw her shoulders finally slump as if in defeat. "Ms. Rutherford I suppose?"

"Yes."

"It was going to be a family only thing." She hedged.

"Really, Mother? No one else was invited?"

She frowned at him and grabbed her purse from the table. "Fine, bring her if you must. I guess we'll put up with anything to see you."

And he'd have to put up with anything to see them. But he was willing to make the effort. They were the only parents he had. After walking his mother to the door, he leaned down to kiss her on the cheek.

"I never said thank you for everything you did for me, especially at the hospital. I just want you to know, I appreciate it."

For a second she looked astonished, then grateful. Maybe his parents weren't the only ones with high expectations. "There's no need to thank us. You're our son; of course we would help you get away from that awful place. I just thank God every day you're home now." She patted his hand. "I'll see you Sunday at five o'clock."

As he watched her walk down the steps and out to her car, he realized that even though she didn't always understand him, she did love him. And in the long run that was more important than anything else.

Opening the French doors, he watched as Kena walked around the shallow end of the pool. She wandered aimlessly as if lost in thought. Her melancholy gave her an air of mystery as she tilted her head back to allow the sun to shine on her face.

When he'd arrived home he'd been excited to talk to her, but as soon as he'd seen his mother's car he'd realized there was going to be trouble. He had to give Kena her due though. She'd remained calm and held her own against his mother. He knew he was falling for her for a reason.

"I guess I missed a lot of your conversation with my mother?"

Kena turned with a look of shock and dismay on her face. That didn't bode well.

"What did you overhear?"

"Nothing much, just something about you caring for me and then you mentioning she's a bit controlling." Baldwin thought that was an understatement. He settled himself on one of the chaise lounges. Although his leg was healing, he still had to rest it every now and then.

Her face looked stricken as she walked toward him. "I didn't mean to insult your mother."

"Baby, I don't know what went on between you and my mother, but please, come on over here." He held out his hand and pulled her onto the lounger with him, settling her between his thighs. With her back to his chest, he wrapped his arms around her. "Now talk."

"I don't know how to keep my mouth shut. I probably said some stuff I shouldn't have but she was just so..."

"I know you speak your mind and I know my mother can be controlling, so I can only imagine what was said." She turned in his arms until she could look him in the face. She seemed as if she wanted to interrupt him, but he held up his hand. Tilting her head toward him, he kissed her soundly.

"Okay, you can't leave me hanging, what did she say?"

"She wanted to know how I was doing and invited me to dinner next Sunday."

Disbelief tainted her voice. "That's it?"

"Oh yeah, you're invited to Sunday dinner too." How the invitation was extended wasn't really all that important.

Pulling her back into his arms, he relaxed against the cushions.

"You're kidding?"

"Nope, five o'clock Sunday, hope you're free."

Kena turned on her side, her fingers playing with the buttons on his shirt. "I'm not too sure what I think about going to dinner at your parents' house. Do you think she'll try to poison me?"

He laughed out loud. "If you go with me I'll promise to switch my plate with yours."

"I'll think about it."

"So, do you want to hear about my morning?"

"Uh, yeah, sure."

"I met with a lawyer and I set up a foundation for veterans. I used the bulk of the money I had left from my grandpop's estate. The money will go to making improvements at the VA hospitals."

"Oh, Baldwin, that's great." She sat up and turned to him, hugging him tightly.

"It won't be a lot at first. He had some money, but I'm no multi-millionaire. But I figure we can use this as a base and then start having fundraisers to add to the foundation."

"I think you'd be surprised at how many people would want to contribute to this cause."

"I made myself the chair of the foundation so I can ensure the money goes where it will most be needed. And I thought I could fill the rest of the positions with displaced veterans."

"It sounds like you put a lot of thought into this."

She had no idea. When she'd challenged him to stop feeling sorry for himself, he began to look at his life and what he'd done with it since he'd been discharged. And he didn't like what he saw. The only bright spot during that time had been Kena. He took her advice and found a way to put the money he'd resented to good use.

"I just want you to know, none of this would have been possible without you. You were the impetus to get me out of my funk and started down this road. I can't thank you enough."

She smiled up at him and then started to look thoughtful. "I know you said you realize I speak my mind."

"Yes."

"And I know it's probably none of my business." He'd finally figured out that would never stop her.

"But..."

"Have you thought any more about contacting your friends?"

Contacting them, no. But when planning for the foundation he'd thought about them a lot, even going so far as to pull out the old photograph. He knew for a fact none of them were living in town right now, but it wasn't as if he didn't have the means to track them down.

"Not really, although now that you mention it --"

"I just thought they might be interested in this project you're doing. They're all veterans, right?"

"Yeah."

"So, what do you think?"

"I think with you by my side I can do just about anything. Even convince you to talk to me about the whole you-caring-for-me thing."

She opened her mouth and then closed it again before wrapping her arms around his neck. "Convince me how?"

"Tie you to my bed?"

"Been there, done that. Got anything else?"

"Hmm, how about I give you free and unlimited access to my body whenever you like?"

She leaned forward and kissed him. "Although I like that idea, I think I could probably get that out of you anyway."

"Found out," he replied in mock horror.

"I have an idea though."

Smiling he wondered where her devious little mind was going. "Do tell."

"How about I get to speak my mind, tell you what I think you ought to do, and the only punishment I get is a spanking at my request?"

"Now that I can do."

Epilogue

Baldwin nervously paced the length of the room as he waited for Kena to finish dressing. They had arrived in Chicago the day before and checked into the Ritz-Carlton, but instead of sightseeing, they'd enjoyed dinner in the room and an evening in. Then they continued their lovefest with room service and breakfast in bed. She'd finally pulled him out of the room and they'd taken a walk around the city that afternoon before returning to get ready for the evening.

As he reached the window, high above the city, he stared out at the lights twinkling in the night. Although he'd never voiced his concerns out loud, somehow she'd known he was nervous about seeing his friends again. Nervous about how things would be after all these years. After the first initial contact to set up the meeting he didn't really mention the reunion. Only after actually seeing the three men would he be able to judge if they were still the same friends he'd known in high school. He hoped this would be the beginning of continued contact and he wouldn't let them drift out of his life again so easily.

"Baldwin, could you help me?"

Turning, he came to a halt as Kena walked toward him. She was perfection. The color of her jade green dress showed off her mocha skin, but it was the cut that showed off her body. The material clung suggestively to her curves and the crisscross over her breasts only accentuated her firm globes. All worries of meeting his friends fled his mind as he wondered if she were wearing any panties under the silky material.

"I can practically feel you undressing me with your eyes."

"Not undressing, just wondering what's on underneath."

She smiled seductively, then slowly pulled the skirt of her dress up, exposing thigh high stockings. She had gorgeous legs and the short skirt showed them off well. But what really caught his eye was her bare mound. She'd recently gotten waxed and he was happily enjoying the benefits on this trip. He moaned appreciatively, remembering licking her awake this morning.

"Damn woman, I'm not going to be able to remember a word said tonight. I'll be dreaming of eating your pussy."

"Drinks first, you can 'eat' later." She handed him her necklace before turning her back to him and lifting her hair.

He quickly hooked the necklace around her before licking the soft spot exposed just behind her ear. She shivered as he pulled her back into his arms.

"So I can't talk you into a quickie before we head to the bar?"

"Hmm --" her head lolled back against his shoulder as she seemingly considered his request -- "as nice as that sounds, we need to meet your friends."

"Are you sure I can't convince you?" His hand pulled the material at her waist until her legs and pussy were once again exposed. She spread her legs, allowing him access. He reached between her thighs, teasing at her bare mound.

"We're going to be late." Her words were denying him, but her body was not. Her lips were slick with her desire as he teased at her seam before pressing a finger inside.

"It'll be worth it." His finger was joined by another and he began to fuck her with the two digits. Her hips bucked and she moaned appreciatively. He flicked his thumb across the sensitive bundle of nerves at the apex of her thighs and she jerked in his arms. She was more than primed for this.

He pulled his fingers from her body and began to frig her clit. She gripped his arms tightly as her orgasm began to hit. He held her in his arms as her orgasm rocketed through her body. Her head lolled back against his chest as her breathing slowly began to regulate. She tried to turn in his arms, but he held her still. "But you..."

"It's okay, you were right. We're going to be late. Besides, we have the rest of our lives together."

Baldwin picked up her left hand and brought it to his lips, kissing the finger that held her engagement ring. He'd given her his grandmother's ring, a family heirloom she treasured just as much as he did. He'd only asked her to marry him a few weeks ago, but their lives were so closely intertwined it seemed as if they'd been together forever.

In the last six months she'd helped him through his reconciliation with his family and had even become somewhat friendly with his mother. They'd never be close confidantes, but were both willing to get along for his sake. Surprisingly, his father had warmed up to Kena and had become a presence in their lives.

"I can't wait to introduce you to the guys."

She entwined their hands and they headed from the room. They took the elevator to the twelfth floor and entered the Trianon Bar. His gaze swept the room but he didn't recognize anyone. He glanced at his watch and realized they were a little early.

"Hey mister, want to buy me a drink?"

"Anything the lady wants." Smiling down at her, he settled his arm around her and headed toward the bar. He ordered their drinks, but his eyes continued to return to the entrance, waiting for the appearance of his friends.

"Hey, they'll get here. Don't worry."

"I'm not wor --" His words trailed off as a man walked into the room, his arm wrapped around a dark-haired woman.

He would recognize Adam anywhere. The man's blond hair was military cut, but he still looked the same as he had the last time Baldwin had seen him. The woman was a bit of a surprise since Adam had always gone for the tall, slender types in high school. But the content look on his friend's face when he glanced down at the small, curvy woman expressed his happiness.

When Adam finally looked up and caught his gaze, the other man broke out in a welcoming smile. Suddenly all his earlier worries melted away and he couldn't wait until the other two men arrived. They may have all grown older and made some changes in their lives, but these men were still the same friends he'd always known.

Pulling Kena into his arms, Baldwin felt a wave of calmness come over him. He'd rediscovered love, started living again, and reconnected with his friends. He had gone through the fire and come out better than ever, honed by the heat instead of being burned by it.

~ * ~

Liz Andrews

Liz Andrews is a critically acclaimed, multi-published author who enjoys writing erotic romance almost as much as she enjoys reading it. A romantic at heart, Liz is a fierce believer in happily ever after and heroes who make the heart swoon. When not writing, the Ohio native enjoys reading, going to the movies and hosting dinner parties for her friends.

She can be reached at her website www.lizandrews.net or you can email her directly at msliz@lizandrews.net.

RISEN FROM ASH

Rachel Bo

Chapter One: A Chance Observation

Ashland thumbed through her mail as she stepped onto the stair.

"Watch out!"

She glanced up, then dodged quickly aside, pressing her back up against the railing as a packing box tumbled down and hit the bottom tread. The lid flew open, spilling several items onto the cobblestone walkway.

"I'll get it." Ashland tucked her mail and keys into the outside pocket of her purse and stepped down, kneeling to pick up items as heavy footsteps descended toward her.

"That's okay. I'll do it." Masculine fingers appropriated the two books now in her right hand, stuffing them back into the box.

"It's no problem." Smiling, she reached out. "You must be the new neighbor."

The man hesitated for a moment before offering his hand as well. "That's right. Damon Wayland." His fingers closed on hers.

Rough calluses scraped against her palm, unexpectedly raising goose bumps along her spine as he shook her hand briefly, then pulled away. He squatted beside her, head down, seemingly engrossed in the task of getting his belongings back into their box.

"I'm Ashland. Ashland Finn. But my friends call me Ash."

"Nice to meet you," her new neighbor answered without looking up.

She studied him for a moment. Even squatting, he was obviously tall, probably six feet or so. He had a lean, hard body and a rugged jaw, his rough good looks and dark tan set off perfectly by his pale blond hair, cropped close in a military-style haircut, crisp tan slacks, and starched white shirt with buttoned-down collar. A frisson of attraction shivered through her, and she frowned. He obviously hadn't been overwhelmed by her good looks and winning personality, if the way he was avoiding meeting her gaze was any indication, and it irked her when her body reacted this way to guys who were so obviously not interested. "Um, well, I guess I'll head up, if you're sure you don't need any help."

"No, thanks." Again, he didn't even glance her way.

Oh, joy, she thought. *Won't it be nice having such a friendly neighbor?* Irritated, she turned and stalked up the stairs, only realizing when she got to the landing that she was still holding a sports towel in her left hand. "Oh." She leaned over the balcony railing. "Damon!" The guy had just replaced the last item in the carton and was about to tuck the cardboard flaps back into place. He glanced up. "I forgot to give you this." She reached out and tossed the dark blue towel, the lapel pins decorating its length glittering brightly as it arced down in the evening sunlight and landed right on top of the items within the box.

"Hey, good shot!" Her reticent neighbor finally cracked a smile. Nodding his head, he closed the lid and picked up the container as he stood, but still didn't really look at her.

Ashland smiled anyway, her thoughts racing as she turned and let herself into her townhome.

Damon frowned as he made his way back up the steps, wondering if the woman had noticed the titles of the two books she'd been holding. Probably not. *Mastering Bondage* and *Alternative Lifestyles: Contracts for Beginners* -- a book from his early days, but one he hadn't wanted to part with -- surely would have elicited a comment or two, or at the very least some apprehension. Mostly, she'd just seemed irritated that he wasn't responding to her friendly overtures.

At the top of the steps, he shifted the box, supporting it against a windowsill as he opened the front door. Stepping inside, he kicked the door shut behind him, depositing his burden on the couch. "That's the last one," he muttered, surveying the neatly arranged, meticulously labeled containers in the living and dining rooms. "Time to go out and get a bite to eat." When he returned, he'd unpack the bedroom and bathrooms. Tomorrow he'd take care of the living room, den, kitchen, and dining room. Nodding, he turned back toward the door and let himself out.

Ash watched her new neighbor stride down the stairs, graceful and formidable as a jungle cat. Sighing, she let the curtain drop back over the window. She walked into the kitchen and turned on the coffeepot, beginning to relax as the rich scent of hazelnut permeated the air. When it was ready, she poured herself a cup and grabbed the small carton of half-and-half from the fridge. Sitting at the table, she added a teaspoon of sugar, a dollop of cream, and stirred slowly as she considered the evening's encounter.

The man had been almost rude, but she thought she knew why. She chanced a sip of her hot brew, then winced and blew across the liquid surface to cool it.

She hadn't paid attention to whatever else was on the ground, or the books she'd picked up, but the towel was another matter. She'd seen towels like that before -- usually at her niece's softball tournaments. Each team competing at the national tournaments had lapel pins made up, and the girls traded them, fastening the souvenirs to sports towels or lanyards to save.

His was a collection of a very different kind. Ash's hands trembled, her body filled with an almost forgotten longing as she lifted her cup to take another sip. She'd glimpsed only a few of the baubles, gleaming as the towel tumbled in the air, but she was sure there'd been pins featuring the logos of the National Coalition for Sexual Freedom and the Sexual Independence Now organization, and another from a popular BDSM club she'd visited once some time ago, called Original Sin. Most people outside of the lifestyle wouldn't recognize the emblems, but she imagined he'd still be reluctant to flaunt them. It certainly explained the guy's rush to get his things back into the box, and his reluctance to accept help.

She swallowed her coffee, breathing deeply through her nose in an attempt to rein in her excitement. The first two pins didn't necessarily indicate that the guy was into BDSM.

He might be gay or bi or a swinger or any number of other things. But Original Sin...that was a BDSM club. She closed her eyes, imagining how the strong, rough palm that had grasped her hand would feel if it were holding her legs, spreading them apart to cuff her ankles to a couple of sturdy bedposts.

Ash shook her head and sighed. She'd given up on finding the right man, hadn't she? It was stupid to even fantasize, especially about a guy she'd just met. And anyway, he might be a sub. Her instincts told her no, but she'd been wrong before. Just because a person was dominant in their public life didn't mean they were dominant in their private life. *She* was proof of that. In her public life, she owned an independent laboratory which performed testing for almost two hundred small physicians' offices. She worked her butt off to keep quality, speed, and accuracy up and costs down, and hers was one of the few independent laboratories in the state that now operated in the black. No business decision was made without her explicit approval. The rewards, both financial and in knowing that she was doing something good for people, made the venture worthwhile, but she shouldered a huge amount of responsibility and suffered a great deal of stress.

That's why she'd turned to the BDSM community. She'd always been intrigued by the lifestyle, always wondered what it would be like to be completely dominated outside of her public life. The idea of turning herself over to someone else when she came home, someone who would take charge, tell her what to do, not require her to make any more decisions, take some of the weight off her shoulders, had convinced her to do some research. She'd carefully scoured the Internet, joined discussion groups, and read hundreds of bulletin boards, getting a feel for the legitimate organizations and clubs in her area. She'd finally worked up the nerve to join a very discreet group that met in one of the member's houses, a rather large home located about a forty-five-minute drive from San Antonio proper, with a fully equipped dungeon. There, she'd explored many aspects of the different alternative lifestyles and confirmed what she'd already suspected, that outside of working hours, she longed to play a sexually submissive role to a powerful Master.

She'd had high hopes at first, but so far her relationships hadn't worked out. She'd participated in scenes with several Doms at parties, and those had been fun, but she'd wanted something longer term. However, the men she'd been involved with so far had been a big disappointment. She'd included in her contracts the fact that she owned a business and was on call twenty-four hours a day, seven days a week. Keeping her cell phone within reach, allowing her to answer it, and understanding that she would possibly have to leave to deal with a problem on a moment's notice had been the top three items on her list, and each Dom had agreed. When put to the test, though, every one of them had issues with the other demands on her time. What seemed to bother them the most were the brief glimpses of her own dominant nature, as it functioned in the business world. Maybe she'd just chosen the wrong people, but in her experience, Dominants seemed to have difficulty witnessing their sub performing outside that submissive role.

She shrugged. Sometimes, what seemed perfectly acceptable on paper just didn't pan out in real life for the people involved.

She sipped her coffee, savoring the flavor as she pictured her new neighbor's gorgeous eyes. An odd color -- a light brown she'd never seen before, the color of dark honey. She imagined those eyes staring into hers with just the right mixture of desire and reprimand, then mentally gave herself a kick in the butt. Even if the guy *was* a Dom, he wasn't the type to be interested in her. Too attractive by far.

She dumped the dregs of her coffee in the sink and rinsed her cup, then turned off the light, heading for the bedroom. As she stripped down to climb into the shower, a grin tugged at her lips. Oh, well, one good thing had come from the encounter. At the very least, she'd acquired a handsome new face to plug into her nighttime fantasies.

Chapter Two: Memories and Pain

Hey, Damon --

Dude! You're not going to believe this shit! I'm gonna join the fucking MARINES! No lie. I went down and talked to the recruiter this morning. I ain't told my mom yet. I don't know how she's going to take this. But, you know, I don't have any skills and I'm tired of fucking living at home and shit. Besides, you know me, dude. I've always been up for a fucking challenge. And from what I hear, the Marine Corps is the biggest fucking challenge there is.

It seems really right to me to be going into the Marine Corps. After all, from all the fucking sports I've played, I'm sure used to taking fucking orders! More than that, and I know it sounds corny, dude, but I really fucking want to do something to defend this country. I don't want to wave the flag or nothing, but America means something to me, dude. I know you, of all people, can understand that.

When I get to boot camp, I'll write you and let you know how to get in touch with me.
Mike

Damon shook his head. He'd forgotten what mouths he and Mike had when they were in high school. Setting the letter down on his desk, he picked up a framed five-by-seven picture of four grinning teenagers. Mike Collins, Baldwin Garrett, Richard Riley, and he had been nearly inseparable in high school. He studied the old photo and smiled, feeling strangely wistful. It wasn't like him to engage in sentiment, but for the first time in a while, he wondered about the old gang. In the time they'd been friends, they'd learned things about each other that were hidden from the rest of the world, and they never judged, never abandoned. But they did scatter after graduation. Eventually, they'd all ended up in a branch of the Armed Forces. Baldwin joined the Air Force, like Damon, but Rich went into the Army, and Mike had joined the Marines. They'd written each other occasionally, but it had become increasingly difficult to stay in touch, especially after he was deployed to Balad Air Base in Iraq.

The thought of Balad stirred up memories he didn't want to explore. Shaking his head to push away the visions trying to crowd themselves into his mind, he stowed the letter in the top drawer of his desk and placed the picture on the shelf above it. He stared at the happy faces for a moment more. Maybe he'd try to find them. He felt…weightless since he'd been reassigned from Balad to Lackland Air Force Base in San Antonio. His head wasn't screwed on right yet. He'd lost direction, focus. He needed to find an anchor, something --

or someone -- to keep him from drifting. He had a number for Baldwin somewhere, from a couple of years ago. He could call and see if the number was still good. If not, there was always the Internet. Baldwin was an unusual first name; he just might be able to find a listing for his friend.

Later, though. He was almost finished unpacking and didn't want to lose momentum. He picked up the empty box from which he'd been restoring the contents of his desk and broke it down.

A door slammed, startling him. He turned and strode over to the window. His next-door neighbor pounded down the steps and out toward the parking lot, stopping beside a silver minivan. He raised his eyebrows. A minivan? From his brief encounter with her the night before, he wouldn't have pegged her as the minivan type, though at this moment he wasn't sure exactly why he'd think that.

Then again, he decided, taking his first really good look at her as he watched her greet an elderly man walking his dog, *I guess she* is *minivan material.* Somewhat short, maybe five-four, five-five, she appeared to be in her early thirties, around his age, and carried quite a bit of extra weight. She was probably married with three kids, the typical soccer mom.

He hadn't noticed the night before -- if he remembered correctly, she'd had it pulled back -- but the woman had gorgeous hair. A riot of dark brown, slightly curling strands gleamed in the setting sun, spilling down to her waist, auburn highlights glinting with each movement as she gestured animatedly. He let his gaze follow the bright tumble and found himself studying her body. Yes, she was overweight, but after a moment of careful observation, he decided the look suited her. She had a large-boned frame, which the extra pounds rounded out nicely. She'd look terrible without that softening -- gaunt, even.

He let his gaze travel a bit further. Nice wide hips below a defined waistline, shapely legs...as a matter of fact, she had a rather pleasant hourglass figure. The curves of that glass were more ample than he usually preferred, but to his surprise, the warmth of desire flushed his abdomen and set his blood humming.

And the hair...his fingers twitched as he imagined wrapping them in those maple-syrup locks, tugging her back, arching the woman over and --

"No." He pushed away from the window, closing his eyes and rubbing the lids. Hands shaking, he sat abruptly on the couch, trying to get a handle on the nearly overwhelming need that surged through him. God. It had been a while since he'd had such a strong craving to dominate. Sex, yes. He hadn't sworn off women completely -- couldn't, truth be told. But the Mastery, his old life...he wouldn't allow himself that kind of a relationship anymore.

The faces of Balad, men and women who had fought for the United States in Iraq and had been injured, or suffered torture, flickered across his field of vision. Bones broken, bodies scarred. Iraqi civilians, too, their bodies twisted, altered by the American force's artillery shells or their own people's suicide bombs or hidden mines -- they haunted him as well. So much suffering.

So much *pain*.

He groaned and pushed up from the couch, heading for the bathroom, already experiencing the relentless pounding that signaled the onset of a severe migraine. He opened the medicine cabinet and grabbed his medication. Strong stuff, and he normally tried to avoid taking it, but the move, with the memories stirred as he went through each box, had taken a toll on him. Today, he didn't think he could hold the visions back without it. He popped two pills into his mouth, cupped his hands under the faucet, then brought them up and sucked in enough water to get the medication down. Then he headed for the bedroom, closed the door, drew down the blackout shades he'd installed before doing anything else, and collapsed on the bed in utter darkness, praying for sleep to take him quickly.

Chapter Three: In the Still of the Night

Damon sat up, fully alert, knowing instinctively that several hours had passed. He glanced at the digital clock on his nightstand. Eleven-thirty. He listened intently, wondering what had awakened him.

Faintly, keys jingled. He jumped from the bed and headed for the front room.

"So, have you met your new neighbor yet?" a feminine voice asked as two sets of heels clattered up the stairs.

His neighbor -- what was her name? -- snorted, a very unladylike sound. "If you could call it that. He dropped a box at my feet and wouldn't even let me help him pick the stuff up. He hardly looked at me, even when we spoke. I don't think he's the friendly type."

"Too bad."

Damon leaned over the couch, looking out the window. Beneath her porch light, his neighbor and another woman stood as she fitted a key into her front door lock. Despite the fact that he had yet to hang shades or a curtain in here, they didn't notice him, as they were turned slightly away from him on the landing his townhome shared with the neighbor's.

As her door swung open, his neighbor answered, "It sure is, because he's absolutely *gorgeous*. Not that I think he'd be interested in *me*, but it would be nice to be friends just to be able to look at him up close on a regular basis." He glimpsed the corner of her mouth turning up as she flashed a wicked grin.

Her guest giggled as they stepped inside, and then the door shut and he could hear nothing more.

Damon turned and settled into the couch. So, not a soccer mom. At least, he didn't think so. She talked like a single woman and was obviously attracted to him, and it finally occurred to him that he hadn't seen anyone else in and out of the place next door. No other man and certainly no kids. But why the *van?* For some reason, he found himself desperate to know.

Which was ridiculous. Who the hell cared? He shook his head and pushed himself up, heading for the bathroom. He needed a shower and a meal. Then he'd finish unpacking the kitchen stuff and he'd be done.

It was odd, though, and faintly irritating how his mind kept returning to his neighbor. Throughout the shower, the meal, and unpacking, he pushed away a dozen tempting images of the woman in various stages of undress. There was just something about her. She seemed so comfortable with herself.

Maybe…maybe he *should* consider dating again. Sure, he'd given up the BDSM lifestyle, but that didn't mean he couldn't still have a fulfilling relationship. Did it?

A relationship? Damn. He stopped in the middle of opening a box. Sex, okay, but was he really thinking he might want something long term with this girl? With anyone, for that matter?

To his shock, he found himself seriously intrigued by the idea.

Okay. Conversation, companionship, maybe. But the sex he'd had since Balad…the minute things turned physical, he started holding back, afraid to let go, worried that in the heat of passion he might give in to old urges. Damon shook his head. He'd heard of *women* being called frigid, but had never dreamed the adjective would be applied to him. That had happened, though. Twice. And others hadn't enjoyed themselves either, though they'd used the words *mechanical* or *detached* to describe him, rather than *cold*.

His head began to pound. Wincing, he forced his mind to empty, focusing on the task at hand. One step at a time. Forks here, spoons there, glasses in this cabinet. He lost himself in the mundane rhythm of unpacking and forced the shadows, and the temptations, far into the recesses of his mind.

Chapter Four: A Taste of the Good Life

"Oh, hi!"

Damon glanced to his left, where the neighbor woman was aiming a watering nozzle at the plants below his front window.

"I hope you don't mind." She brushed a wisp of hair back from her forehead. "My last neighbor wasn't much into gardening, so I used to water the plants for her. If you'd rather I didn't..." She cocked her head, obviously waiting for a reply.

Damon turned toward her. Half of him wanted to tell her to get the hell away, that he could take care of his own damn yard, but the other half...He stood silent, struggling to make a decision.

She shrugged, her gaze direct and a little angry. "I see. I guess I shouldn't have presumed." She flipped a toggle on the nozzle, interrupting the flow of liquid, then grabbed the hose proper with her free hand and started dragging it back across the walkway.

Damon reached out, fingers closing on her upper arm. "No! I mean, it's all right."

Her gaze darted to his hand. His tan from the flight line stood out dark against her lighter, golden skin.

He let go immediately. "Really. Watering the grass and mowing's about all I'm good for."

She hesitated, a tentative smile curling the edges of her lips. "Are you sure?

Damon nodded. "Yeah. Look, I'm sorry if I appeared…" He couldn't find an appropriate word, and shook his head. "What did you say your name was?"

The woman tilted her head, studying him for a long moment before answering. "Ashland. But my friends call me Ash."

Staring into her brown eyes, with the morning sun picking out flecks of green in their depths, he found himself saying, "And am I a friend?" Despite his best intentions, he couldn't resist flirting with her.

Ashland grinned impishly. "I hope so. Neighbors should be friends, I think."

Her good humor was infectious. Damon felt the corners of his lips rising. "Makes life easier," he observed.

Ash nodded and turned away, aiming her nozzle at the far corner of the flowerbed. She flipped the toggle back. Water surged from the hose again, then settled into a gentle patter. The earthy scent of damp loam drifted over him.

A need to keep the moment going nearly overwhelmed him. What the heck was going on? He'd had only two brief encounters with the woman -- four if he counted watching her through the window and eavesdropping the night before. He knew absolutely nothing about her, except that she was exceptionally friendly. And forgiving. He could admit to himself that he'd been downright rude the day she'd tried to help him, and yet here she was watering his plants, even after he'd acted the tongue-tied moron.

And he, for some unfathomable reason, was reacting like a boy in the grip of his first teenage hormones.

Decision time, Damon. He started to turn away. It wouldn't be good to get involved with a neighbor. If it didn't work out, they'd both end up miserable. But Ash bent over, nipping a spent blossom from one of the neatly trimmed rosebushes with two fingernails, and Damon froze. Friendly, helpful, and hot *damn*, what an ass! His pulse quickened, the heat of desire flooding his veins. What *was* it about the woman? She wasn't even his usual type, for God's sake!

But how could he ignore what his body was telling him? Nothing had piqued his interest -- or his libido -- for quite some time. He took a deep breath. Okay, so *one* date. Just something to get his feet wet. Something harmless, like --

"Ash?"

"Hmm?" She straightened, heading for the faucet, where she turned the water off and began wrapping up the hose as she raised her gaze to his.

"Have you had breakfast yet?"

She seemed shocked, eyebrows raised. Her hands stilled and she stared at him, uncharacteristically speechless.

"That's twice you've helped me out, now. I'd like to buy you breakfast. As a thank you." Not completely honest, but now that he was actually responding to her, she looked like a deer caught in headlights. Had he really been that awful to her?

"Umm." She glanced down at her hands, abruptly tossing the coiled hose aside. "Breakfast sounds great, actually." She gestured toward her home. "Could you give me a moment?"

He nodded, sliding his hands into his pockets. Ash jogged quickly up the stairs and disappeared behind her door.

Inside the house, Ash picked up her cell phone and dialed as she headed toward the kitchen to wash her hands. "Penny? Hey, it's Ash."

A shrill voice asked if she knew it was seven-thirty on frickin' *Sunday* morning.

"I know, I know. I'm sorry. But the guy next door asked me out, and I didn't want to go --"

She held the phone away as cursing changed to a sharp squeal. "The new guy? He asked you out?"

Ash laughed. "Well, it's not exactly a date, I don't think. I was watering his plants this morning, and he said he wanted to thank me, and invited me to breakfast." An abbreviated version, but she'd fill her best friend in on the particulars later. After all, Damon was waiting. "Anyway, since I don't really know him, I didn't want to go without letting someone know where I'd gone and who I was with."

Penny had finally calmed down, sounding wide awake now. "The guy's name was Damon, right?" A good friend for a sub to have, Penny knew exactly what to ask.

"Yes. Damon Wayland." Ash had committed his name to memory the moment he introduced himself that first day. She was vaguely disappointed he hadn't done the same for her, but hey, he was taking her to breakfast, wasn't he? "Listen, I've got to go. He's waiting. You know his address; he lives right next door. If you don't hear from me by, say, ten o'clock, send the cavalry."

"Wait! Where are you guys going?"

"Oh." Ash frowned. "Hang on a sec." She walked over to the front door and opened it. "Damon, did you have some place in particular in mind?"

He shrugged. "I don't know this part of San Antonio that well yet, but I know there's an IHOP near the interstate." He raised his eyebrows in a questioning manner.

"IHOP sounds great." She stepped back into the living room and grabbed her purse and keys. "You got that, right?" she asked Penny.

"Got it. Hey, have fun! And don't you dare forget to call me."

"I won't. Gotta run." Ash flipped her phone closed and tucked it into a pocket on the side of her purse. Stepping outside, she pulled the door shut and locked it.

Ashland was breathless when she rejoined him on the walkway. Damon quirked an eyebrow. "Letting someone know where you'll be?"

Her cheeks flushed rosy again, but she didn't look away. "Well, yeah. I mean --"

He held up a hand. "Don't worry. I'm glad. Let's face it, you don't know me from" -- he grinned -- "well, from Damon."

Ashland laughed, a deep, rich sound, pleasantly startling. "True."

Damon led the way to his Jeep, frowning as he opened the door for her. "You'd probably like the top on."

"Are you kidding? On such a gorgeous morning?" She shook her head. "What's the use of having a car like this if you can't enjoy it?"

His sentiments exactly, but not many of the women he'd dated felt that way. Usually, if he left the top off, they worried about their hair during the whole ride.

To his delight, Ash wasn't like that at all. She smiled and leaned into the breeze, appearing to enjoy the wind rushing past. She didn't try to force conversation either, content to let him drive while she watched the passing scenery.

Once they were inside the restaurant and had placed their orders, she sat back and regarded him frankly. "So, which branch of the military?"

Damon chuckled. "How'd you know?"

"It's the way you carry yourself, I think. My dad and granddad are both retired military. You remind me of them."

He nodded. "Makes sense. I'm Air Force, stationed at Lackland."

"Just now?" She flashed a smile at their waitress as the woman delivered their drinks.

Damon took a sip of his orange juice, then set it aside. "Actually, no. I've been at Lackland for a couple of years, living on base. But I'm going to be here a while, so I decided it was time for something...I don't know. A little more private, I guess. Less like a hotel room, more like a home."

Ash nodded in understanding. Their eyes met, and Damon stared into hers, thinking again how beautiful they were, so bright and open, with flashes of green glinting in their bronze depths.

She blushed and turned her head, staring out the window, apparently embarrassed by this deep scrutiny.

"Are you married?" Damon blurted out.

She took in a quick breath and turned back to him. "No."

"Boyfriend?"

Maybe the red in her cheeks hadn't been embarrassment, as he'd assumed, because she met his gaze without the slightest bit of coy reluctance. "No." She tilted her head, her expression bold and openly curious. "Why?"

Damon reached out to where her hands rested clasped upon the table. He tugged one loose, turning it so that it faced upward, then lightly drew his fingertips across her palm. She shivered, and her cheeks reddened again, but she didn't look away. So. Not embarrassed, after all.

Turned on.

"I think you know," he said.

She frowned, but didn't pull away. "Honestly, I'm confused."

"Confused?"

The waitress appeared with their meals. At that, she *did* start to pull away, but Damon tightened his grip. After a slight hesitation, she relaxed, leaving her fingers wrapped in his.

"Just set them there, thanks." Damon smiled and waited while the woman deposited their plates. After she'd retreated, he turned his attention back to Ashland. "Confused?" he prompted again.

Ash nodded. "Friday, when you were moving in, I got the distinct impression you weren't interested in me in the slightest. Not even as a neighbor you would wave to in passing. As a matter of fact, I thought you would have preferred not to have met me at all."

Damon frowned, at a loss as to what to say. He couldn't tell her, *Oh, well, that was just because I didn't want you to see the BDSM paraphernalia in that box*. He decided to improvise. "I know. Look, I'm sorry. That was the last box. I'd been moving all day, and by that time I was tired and hungry and not in a very good mood." All of which was true, actually.

He slid his hand along hers, cupping her forearm and rubbing his thumb gently across the pulse point at her wrist. She shivered again in response, though she appeared to realize what was happening and stiffened quickly, trying to hide it. "But Saturday morning, I saw you again from my window, speaking with an older man who was walking his dog. I took a good long look, and something clicked. After that, I couldn't stop thinking about you."

Her flesh was warm in his. He raised her hand and turned it, brushing his lips ever so lightly across her knuckles, his gaze never leaving hers.

Her eyes widened. She took a deep breath, then blurted, "Why?"

"I don't know," he answered honestly. "But I'd like to find out."

Ashland snorted, eyeing him suspiciously. "Damn. If that's a line, it's a good one."

He laughed. "Well, I'll tell you up front..." He leaned even closer to her, enjoying the banter. Her eyes were glued to his, her palm sweaty, her pulse racing. He felt a surge of satisfaction. He knew, though she hadn't said it yet. He could feel in his bones that the answer was going to be yes -- to dating, to *him*. They'd known each other all of thirty minutes, and he was already in control. It was a rush, almost as invigorating as a good D/s session. Maybe he couldn't return completely to his old lifestyle, but would a bit of psychological domination cause any harm? Maybe he didn't need the sexual D/s to get back on an even keel.

Maybe.

Ashland waited, brow furrowed, for him to finish his thought. He flashed a wicked grin. "My intentions are absolutely *not* honorable," he growled.

She wanted him. He could see it in her eyes. She wanted to say yes, but there was a hint of uncertainty there. Maybe she was afraid of ending up with her heart broken, or maybe she was just worried about getting involved with someone she'd just met, but she wasn't sure what to do.

So he told her. "Say yes, Ash."

As though he'd flipped a switch, her brow smoothed. "Yes, Damon," she whispered.

A thrill of triumph swept through him. Damn! He hadn't been this assertive with a woman since...well, since about six months into his time in Balad. That's when he'd started questioning his lifestyle. He'd toned himself down, started letting the woman take the initiative, even though that wasn't really his nature.

This... *this* felt good. Familiar.

Right.

Damon sat back in the booth, letting go of her hand reluctantly. He smiled, and she grinned back.

Decision made, she seemed completely at ease. No regrets, no lingering concerns. She raised her eyebrows, darting her gaze to their plates. "Our food's getting cold."

"Mm-hmm." Damon continued looking at her, enjoying the slight flush that rose in her cheeks, traveling down her neck, kissing the bit of cleavage her V-neck tee revealed.

"Damon," she murmured, sweeping her gaze out across the restaurant as though to ask what people would think.

He didn't care what they were thinking, but he *was* hungry -- for more than just breakfast. "You'll kiss me later." He made it a statement, not a question, just to see how she'd react.

She took a deep breath, then let it out slowly, nodding. "If that's what you want."

"It is," he said and pushed their platters over so they could eat.

By the time they'd finished breakfast, he'd discovered her parents were retired and living in Galveston, she had two brothers who also lived in San Antonio, and she ran her own business. This last revelation surprised him because he suspected more and more, through his observation of subtle cues and the way she responded to his mild, still somewhat experimental assertions of authority, that she was a natural submissive. He wouldn't have thought running a business would be something that would appeal to a sub. Then again, he'd mainly met subs through the BDSM network. He hadn't wanted long-term relationships at the time, so he'd mostly done scenes and short-term contracts. He hadn't bothered with finding out much about the type of person they were outside their time with him. But he *had* heard over the years that many submissives were actually in positions of authority in the business world. His friend Brian had mentioned one time that those subs craved the private role reversal, to alleviate the pressure they experienced in their public life and release stress.

"Will there be anything else?" Their waitress was at his elbow. He'd been watching Ash finish her coffee, thinking while he waited. He glanced up and shook his head. "No, thank you."

She tugged the ticket from her waistband and slapped it on the table. "There you go." Confiscating their empty plates, she bustled toward the kitchen.

"Are you ready?" he asked Ashland.

She nodded, picking up her purse and scooting out of the booth. Damon guided her to the cash register with a hand at the small of her back. She looked up at him and flashed a quick smile.

After he paid, as they headed for the car, he let his hand slide around her waist. She took a step closer to him, nestling comfortably in the curve of his arm. His pulse quickened. At the car, he turned to her abruptly, drawing her to him, claiming her mouth with his.

Her lips tasted of cinnamon and coffee laced with sugar and cream. Her hands circled his waist, gliding up to cup his shoulder blades. He flicked his tongue between her lips, heat flooding his groin as she sighed and leaned into him. He wrapped his arms around her, deepening the kiss, exploring the soft contours of her mouth, her tongue. The smooth edges of her teeth.

He watched her -- her eyes closed, cheeks flushed -- as his tongue stroked hers. Her eyelids fluttered, her body trembling. His cock strained against his slacks, and he tightened his arms, pulling her close, letting her feel the hard length of him against her rounded belly.

He flicked the tip of his tongue back and forth along the underside of hers. Ash made a desperate sound in the back of her throat. Her fingers curled against his shoulder blades, clutching the fabric of his shirt. Instinctively, he gripped her waist, supporting her as her knees went soft. She was so responsive, as if she were fucking *made* for him! A shudder rippled through him.

He had to have her.

Groaning, he reluctantly relinquished her lips, still holding her close. Ash moaned, opening her eyes. "God." She met his gaze, her own full of cautious wonder. "Is this real, or am I dreaming?"

Damon pinched her butt playfully.

"Oh!" Ash's eyes widened in surprise.

"So you felt that?"

She laughed. "Yes. I guess you're telling me I'm *not* dreaming."

Damon bent his head, bringing his lips close to her ear, and spoke soft and low. "I'm telling you I'm going to take you home now. When we get there, you're going to invite me in, and I'm going to undress you. And then..." He let his voice trail away suggestively.

"Yes, Damon," she breathed out.

He opened the passenger door, and she slid into the seat.

Chapter Five: Simple Matters

Ash cursed twice, fumbling as she attempted to unlock her front door.

"Here." Damon held out his hand, and she dropped her keys into it. He picked out the one she'd been using. Inserting it smoothly into the keyhole, he turned his wrist and pushed.

The door swung open. Ash made an exasperated sound. "I feel like an idiot," she said as he removed the key and handed the key ring back to her.

"You shouldn't." He ushered her inside and shut the door behind them. He turned a knob near the top, the deadbolt hissing as it slid into place. "It's sexy," he insisted as he swiveled and faced her. "Knowing how much you want me."

She drew in a sharp breath, turning her gaze to the floor.

"Don't." He cupped her chin, applying gentle pressure until she raised her head and met his gaze. "I like it when you look me in the eye."

He released her chin, his gaze locked with hers as he let his hands travel the length of her arms. He tugged the keys from her unresisting hand and tossed them onto a small table beneath the mirror hanging in her foyer, then took the purse from her other hand and dropped it to the floor. Grasping her hands, he lifted them above her head.

Without prompting, Ash held the pose when he let go. Reaching down, he slipped his fingers beneath her shirt, gliding them up along the curve of her belly, over the mounds of her silk-clad breasts, drawing the blouse up and off.

Her breathing quickened, her face flushed as she watched him. He reached behind her, deftly unfastening her bra and guiding it over her arms, then letting it fall to the ground. He turned her until she was facing the mirror. "Watch," he whispered in her ear. He traced the borders of her areolas with the tips of his fingers. Her gaze dropped to where her breasts were reflected in the mirror.

Her nipples plumped slightly.

"You like that." He flicked the pads of his index fingers across the peaks of her nipples. The protrusions swelled further, growing stiff at his touch. "Mmm. I can't wait to taste them." She shuddered. "You want that, don't you."

It wasn't really a question, but she raised her eyes to his and nodded.

His cock ached. He didn't know how long he could wait. He dropped his hands to her waist. She had on button-fly jean shorts. Damn, buttons took too long!

He undid the first two quickly, but the third button wouldn't slip through. Frustrated, he gripped each side above it and pulled.

Ash gasped as the last four buttons popped loose, clattering against the floor.

"Take them off," he growled.

Ash pushed the jeans down, shimmying as she worked them over her hips, taking her underwear down with them.

"Yes." He knelt, gliding his hand up between her thighs. She hastily moved one foot to the side, opening herself to him.

His fingers found her slit.

He had meant to take her slow and easy. Tease her for a while, savoring every moment.

He couldn't. He had to feel her. Had to make her hidden parts *his*.

He shoved two fingers inside her.

Good God. Her slick warmth surrounded him. Her pussy sucked at his fingers as he pressed inward. She was so *tight*. He wrapped an arm around her waist, holding her as he worked his fingers deeper.

He saw her eyes in the mirror, glazed and dark with need, and his breath caught. He flexed his fingers. Wiggling, searching, he watched her reflection until her eyelids jerked wide and she gasped.

Immediately, he pressed the tips of his fingers into that spot again and again.

Ash breathed hard, rotating her hips slightly, glancing back at him, her gaze beseeching. "That's it, baby," he murmured, palpating her sweet spot. He slid the hand at her waist over the swell of her tummy and down into the red-brown curls between her legs, finding her clit.

"Damon!"

He rubbed the swollen nub, his fingers plunging in and out of her pussy as she rocked her hips.

"Oh, God." She stiffened abruptly.

Damon shoved his fingers as deep as they would go right before her thighs came together, trapping him inside her. "Damon, yes!" she screamed.

He watched her in the mirror, his cock throbbing. Her mouth opened as though she would cry out, but no sound escaped. Glazed and unfocused, her eyes seemed to look through the mirror, to some hidden place, as she shuddered repeatedly.

Her pussy contracted, her flesh slick and warm.

He waited, and as the shuddering spasms began to weaken, he dug the tips of his fingers into her sweet spot again.

She gasped, ripping her gaze from the reflection. Back arching, she closed her eyes, the muscles in her pussy squeezing tight again. "God, yes, Damon. Yes!"

He pulled his left hand away from her clit and pressed it against her back, urging her to bend forward.

She did, hands gripping the edge of the table beneath the mirror.

He stood, the fingers of his right hand still working inside her as he unbuckled his belt with his free hand and shoved his pants down past his hips. He wanted desperately to pound into her. He wanted those lips stretched around him.

She was so tight. He thought it might have been a while since she'd had sex, or possibly her partners had not been very generously endowed.

He, however, was long and thick, thicker than average. If he entered her hard and fast, without preparation, it would hurt.

His blood heated at the thought. He imagined her whimpering. Hurting, but begging him not to stop, because it felt so good.

He imagined slamming into her. Grabbing her nipples, pinching and twisting while he fucked her from behind as she gasped and screamed, coming over and over in spite of -- no, *because* of -- the pain.

A face flashed before his eyes. A young Army grunt, features twisting in agony as Damon helped carry him onto a plane for air evacuation to a hospital that could better deal with his severed leg and multiple shrapnel wounds.

He shuddered, flashing from hot to cold in an instant.

His fingers inside Ashland stilled. Her gasps slowed, her thighs spreading slightly as she relaxed, her orgasm fading.

He withdrew his fingers from inside her, sitting hard on the wooden floor of the foyer. His cock had gone limp. It still throbbed, but unpleasantly, not reacting well to the sudden change.

Ashland stood slowly, turning to look at him uncertainly. "Damon?"

He shook his head and closed his eyes, not knowing what to say, not wanting to see the contempt or pity she might reveal.

He sensed her kneeling beside him. "Just tell me this," she said, her voice trembling. "Is it me?"

She was so nice, so sweet. He'd really wanted to try building a relationship with her. "No, it's not you."

He started as a warm hand cupped his cheek, soft lips brushing his.

He opened his eyes.

Ash met his gaze. She moved in front of him. Reaching out, she slipped his tan dress shoes from his feet.

She grasped the waistband of his pants where it lay gathered at his knees, flashing him a questioning look.

He searched her eyes for any sign of pity or regret, contempt or derision.

He'd never known a person's look could say so much, but everything she felt was there, in her eyes. Her desire exposed to him, raw and powerful. His pulse quickened. He nodded his head, once.

Ash tugged his pants down, pulling them off his legs. She worked his socks off, tucking them inside his shoes and pushing those to the side.

He reached up, unfastening the buttons of his shirt while Ashland watched. When he was done, she slid her hands under the fabric, brushing it aside, pushing it down his arms to puddle against the floor.

He pulled his hands free.

Ash went down on all fours. She pressed her lips against him, planting a kiss in the arch of his foot.

She pressed another kiss to the top of his foot, then his ankle. Heat raced up his leg with each touch.

He drew in a sharp breath, relief and pleasure flooding him as his cock twitched, responding.

She switched sides, treating his right foot to the same pleasures.

She kissed her way up his shins, pushing his legs apart, trading kisses from side to side as she crawled up between them. His cock swelled, stiffening.

When she reached his knees, she guided them up so that the soles of his feet rested against the floor, and spread his thighs wide.

Her lips brushed feather-light along the insides of his thighs.

"Wait."

He scooted back until his spine met the wall behind him, offering some support, then opened his legs wide for her again.

This time, she opened her mouth and pressed her lips tight against him, the tip of her tongue dancing against his skin as she sucked her way up each side to his groin. "Good God." He groaned.

She grinned, looking up at him as she swirled her tongue in a figure eight, its tip circling one ball, coming down between them, circling the other.

"Ash." He wanted desperately to reach out and grab her braid. To tug her up and thrust his cock into her mouth, holding her firm, her hair wrapped around his hand as he thrust, burying himself deep in her throat.

Because he wanted it so bad, he didn't do it.

He wasn't sure if he was afraid it would spark another unpleasant vision, or if he was afraid, if he took the initiative again, that he might lose control. It had been so long since he'd made love the way he needed to.

Ash's lips kissed the dome of his cock. His hands ached to move, to push her down on him, but instead he flattened his palms hard against the floor.

Heat flooded his groin as she stretched her mouth around him, her tongue circling, teasing the edges of the ridge left by his circumcision.

He closed his eyes, then opened them again, afraid of what he might see in that dark. *No more visions*, he begged of the higher power. *And please, God, let me come*, he thought. It had been so long…

Her fingers crept between his buttocks and the floor, kneading his cheeks as she worked her lips down around him. He gasped, thrusting involuntarily.

She moaned, taking him deep, the back of her tongue pressing up against his swollen head. *Oh, God.* His cock thrummed.

And then she moved. Up, then down. Shallowly at first, then deeper and deeper, her teeth scraping the length of his shaft lightly as her pace quickened.

He wanted to, *had* to, reach out and take control of that rhythm.

No.

His fingertips ached where he pressed them tight against the flooring. His muscles trembled with the strain of holding himself back.

He was so focused on not giving in to his need to take control that when the orgasm came, it shocked the hell out of him.

Fire burst in his groin. A surge of heat and pleasure ripped through his cock.

Ash moaned. She pulled her head back, tongue flicking the length of his shaft, then went down again, sucking hard.

Before he could stop himself, Damon arched, thrusting roughly. Ash took him as deep as she could, swallowing, sucking, tongue working, drinking as he poured his essence into her. He tilted his head back and groaned-growled-roared, a primal, inarticulate sound of pleasure and release.

She stayed with him, taking it all. And when it was over, she rested her head on his hip, licking the tip of his cock, sipping up the tiny bits of liquid that continued to seep out slowly.

He winced as he moved his hand. He'd been pressing so hard, restraining himself, that his fingers were stiff and sore. He brushed the wisps of hair that had come loose from her braid back from her temple with the backs of his fingers. "Thank you."

She smiled up at him. "My pleasure."

"Come here."

She sat up. He pulled her toward him, moving her legs to either side so that she straddled him. He kissed her, a chaste, sweet kiss, then guided her arms around him, molding her body to his so that the top of her head tucked in beneath his chin, her cheek resting against his chest. He caressed her back, his cock nestled in her curls, and felt a contentment he'd never felt before.

It lasted until her purse started ringing.

"Shit." Ash pulled her arm free and glanced at her watch. She gave Damon an apologetic look as she disentangled herself, reaching for the strap of her purse. "I have to get that. It's Penny, checking on me. I told her to call at ten if she hadn't heard from me."

He nodded, trying to retain the feeling of ease, but already the doubts and questions were crowding in. *What the hell am I doing? It was too good. It can't possibly last.*

If we ever do this again, there's no way I'll be able to keep from hurting her.

That last was the kicker, and he pushed himself up from the floor as she spoke into the phone.

"Yeah, I'm home." A pause. "Sorry, I just came through the door." Another pause. "Actually, he's not such a jerk after all." She flashed him a grin as she said this.

He picked up his pants, straightened his underwear inside them, and tugged them on. He grabbed his shirt and socks and stepped into the room off the foyer.

Just inside the archway was a recliner. He sat down and pulled on his socks.

"Okay, yeah," he heard Ash say. "I'll call you back later."

She came into the room carrying her clothes, still without a stitch on. She tossed the items onto the couch and sat down, watching him.

He slipped into his shirt and started buttoning it.

"Can I do that for you?"

He hesitated. "Uh, I guess."

She came over and knelt before him, working from the bottom up, her mouth curved by a soft smile. She left the last button undone. "Could you stand?"

He did, and she tucked his tails into his pants, fastening the waistband and pulling up the zipper, her eyes bright and happy. She straightened his left sleeve, which had gotten folded up at some point, and smoothed a wrinkle out of the zipper flap of his pants, all the while radiating an obvious sense of delight.

Damn. He'd been ready to say, "Thanks for the ride," and slip away, making it clear he didn't intend to be anything but neighbors from this point on. Not that he really felt that way, but in order to save her from...well, from *him*.

However, many women had taken his clothes off, and that was certainly erotic, but none of that even began to compare to the way having Ash put his clothes *on* was affecting him.

He was in deep trouble.

He grabbed her hands. "Ash."

She looked up at him with her beautiful brown eyes. "Yes?"

"Next Friday night, seven o'clock. Dinner and a movie."

"Yes, Damon."

He pulled her against him, kissing the corner of her mouth, her cheek, the lobe of her ear. "Wear something clingy," he murmured. "No bra -- I want to be able to see what your nipples are doing."

She swallowed hard. "Yes, Damon."

He wanted very much to stay, but he had to get out. Put the reins on before he saw her again.

He gently disengaged, heading for the door. She padded after him -- when had her sneakers come off? -- and watched while he slipped his shoes on.

Still naked, she stood in the doorway as he stepped out. "Ash?" He tilted his head outward, indicating the street, the neighborhood.

"I don't care." She grinned impishly. "I want this to be the image you take home with you."

"Good God, woman." He groaned. "You're killing me."

"We don't *have* to wait until Friday…"

He nodded. "Yes, we do. Trust me."

"I do."

The simple statement set a lump in his throat. He kissed her goodbye without another word and strode across the landing, not trusting himself to look back.

Chapter Six: Contemplations

Ashland shut the door reluctantly. "Oh. My. God!"

She whirled around, dancing her way into the living room. He *was* nice, after all, and the *body*. Long, lean, hard, and muscular.

She couldn't believe he was really interested in her. Oh, she wasn't modest. Though a large woman, she knew she was pretty. Still, because of the way he'd acted that first day, she hadn't imagined anything like *this* would happen between them. And to be honest, even though she was attractive and had been hit on by her fair share of men, he was way better-looking than the majority of the guys she'd dated. She figured the women on his arm had been mostly tall and slender or tiny and petite. Not someone like her, short but not short enough to be considered tiny, and definitely not petite.

Then again, she'd never had any problems attracting men. They weren't bad lookers, either, just no one quite so high on the gorgeous scale. But she hadn't been interested lately. For about five years, actually. When her D/s partners hadn't worked out, she'd kind of given up. She'd realized quickly, trying to make connections after her BDSM experiences were behind her, that a traditional type of male/female relationship just wasn't going to work for her.

She and Damon had something more going on. Instinctive and natural. Neither of them had been looking for this, she was sure. Yeah, she'd thought he was hot that first day, but uninterested and maybe a bit out of her league, so she hadn't even been trying to connect with him. She'd just been herself, and they'd ended up together. Like they were made for each other.

She collapsed onto the couch. It had felt so good to have something besides a vibrator inside her, even though it was just his fingers.

If only he'd taken her the way she'd hoped. Hard and rough, from the back. He was going to, she was sure of it, but then something had happened. He went from sixty to zero in the space of a second.

He was a Dom. Nothing could convince her otherwise. The way he'd acted...he enjoyed telling her what to do, what to wear. He'd known what she wanted, what she *needed*.

If only he'd given it to her.

Why had he held back? It wasn't just the sixty-to-zero thing. He'd restrained himself, barely, while they were on the floor as well. She'd sensed the leashed aggression, felt his tension.

She'd done what she could to let him know she was receptive to his particular leanings, without coming right out and saying, "Hey, I saw your BDSM pins. I'm into that, too." Maybe he'd had a bad experience. Someone who thought she was into the lifestyle, but really wasn't. Or maybe he was just waiting until they knew each other better.

That might be it. Ash nodded. Since they hadn't met through an organization, he might be worried he would scare her off. He had definitely been determined to get out of there, and she didn't think it was because he didn't want her. No, she was pretty confident it was because he *did*, and he wasn't sure he could keep restraining himself.

So, the question for her was, should she tell him she knew what he was into? She frowned. Might move the relationship along a little faster, but that wouldn't necessarily be a good thing. Anticipation could be a heck of an aphrodisiac.

Besides, she was making a lot of assumptions based on a handful of observations. The truth was, she still didn't know anything about him. She'd done most of the talking at the restaurant. Air Force, and stationed at Lackland. That's all she really knew. She didn't even know what he did there.

Maybe that towel didn't even belong to him. Maybe it belonged to a friend. Could be he had no idea where those lapel pins were from, what they meant. He might have a dominant nature, but that didn't mean he was a true Dom.

Better to wait. Let *him* call the shots.

Ash smiled. That's what she wanted, anyway. A man who would take control, give her a break from the pressure of running her own business, the burden of constant decision-making. If he wanted to take it slow, well, that wasn't such a bad thing.

She stretched, yawning, and grabbed her clothes. She needed a distraction, or she would end up sitting there all day, fantasizing about Damon. Might as well get dressed and call Penny.

"Ninety-seven, ninety-eight, ninety-nine, one hundred!" Damon grunted as he finished the last sit-up and lay back against the floor.

Keeping his mind off Ashland had been harder than he would have thought possible. He'd never felt like this before. He kept listening for sounds from the adjoining townhome. This evening, when he'd heard her front door, he'd gone to the window and seen her leaving with the friend from the night before. He wondered where they'd gone, what they were doing.

Whether Ash was thinking about him.

He shook his head and stood. Wired, he couldn't seem to stop moving. He knew what his body wanted -- more Ash.

His head was telling him that he'd be crazy to keep seeing her. If he thought he'd been frustrated before, that was nothing compared to what he was feeling now. It hadn't been easy to give up the D/s life, but he hadn't realized that the only reason he'd managed to make it so far was that he hadn't met the right girl.

Turned out it was much easier to keep his tendencies in check when he didn't really care about the woman.

That's what a lot of people didn't understand about the lifestyle. Though there were definitely bad apples -- as there were in all walks of life -- for those who lived it, the ones who weren't just playing around or experimenting, BDSM wasn't about a Master getting off on another person's pain or subservience, or a sub being hurt or humiliated. As a Dom, he did gain something from knowing that a person was willing to submit to him, but the real rush came from knowing a sub truly wanted what you had to give. *Craved* it. D/s was about both partners being able to provide the person they loved with a need as basic to them as food and water.

Wait a minute.

Love?

He wasn't honestly thinking Ash might be "the one"?

Hell yeah, he was. That was the problem. His head said one thing, but his heart was arguing hell bent for leather for something else. If she was the one, it was going to make things a lot harder. Her mere presence spoke to something deep inside him, the part where all his dark secrets and inner desires dwelled. She brought out what was real in him, and that was something he'd been avoiding for the last three years.

"Aargh!" He growled and rubbed his face. He was so tired. It was eleven-thirty, and he had to be at work at six in the morning.

Okay. He needed to shower, and then he had to get to bed.

Which wasn't as easy as it sounded. Even with the blackout shades down so that not a shred of light entered the room, and his music going, he still tossed and turned until he heard the faint sound of women's voices out front.

For some reason, just knowing she was there, next door, just a few steps and a knock out of reach, calmed him.

God help him if getting through the rest of the week was this hard!

Chapter Seven: Unchained

Ash was a nervous wreck by the time Friday rolled around. She'd spoken to Damon only a couple of times. She knew he left around five-fifteen every morning for work, because she heard him each day and had gotten into the habit of peeking out to get a glimpse of him as he left. He drove a silver Jeep, which, since it had rained on Tuesday, she now knew had a black top. The car was always back in the parking lot when she came home in the evenings. She didn't usually leave for the lab until about eight-thirty, which meant she didn't get home until about six, so they totally missed each other as far as going to and from work was concerned, other than her sneak peeks.

But he *had* been outside one evening when she and Penny were on their way out for dinner. He was coming back from a jog. Tanned and sweating, he and his fantastic bod gave the term "hot hunk" a whole new meaning. She practically had to hold a towel under her friend's chin to keep the drool from hitting the pavement.

He'd been polite, but not overly friendly, when she introduced them. The only other time they'd seen each other, she was watering, and he'd waved to her as he left, maybe going out to eat, maybe taking some other woman out. Who knew?

She shouldn't worry about it. She had no exclusive claim on him. But he hadn't said a word about their date.

God, she hoped he hadn't forgotten.

Or changed his mind.

Standing in front of her closet, she dialed her cell phone. "Pen, *help!*"

"Watcha need, hon?"

"I don't know what to wear."

"Hmm." There was a moment of silence while her friend thought. Thankfully, she took Ash seriously when she said she needed guidance -- again, a great friend to have when you were a sub without a Dom. "Oh! I know. Wear that red knit dress, the one with the black belt. It makes your boobs look huge and your waist about theeees big." She could picture Penny holding her fingers about a half-inch apart to demonstrate.

"Not red. It makes me look like a hooker."

"Only if you go overboard on the makeup."

"Besides, the top blouses out and he --" Shit. She stopped. She hadn't meant to give away the fact that he'd specified any preferences.

"He what?" Her friend's voice took on a cajoling tone. "Ash? Did he say something? He what? Dish, girl!"

She made a face. "He wants me to wear something clingy."

"Oh, he does, does he?" Penny purred. "Mm-mm-mm. Girl, if it doesn't work out between you two, can I --"

"Pen!"

"All right, all right. Just kidding. Um, how about the little black top with the low, rounded neckline? The one with the tiny silver threads worked into it? And the black cargo-type shorts. They're dressy, but casual enough for the movies, and you'll keep cool."

"Yes!" Ash grabbed the shirt from its hanger and opened a dresser drawer. "You're a genius."

"I know. And you should wear that silver link chain belt with it."

"I thought the chain belts were out this season."

"Huh-uh. They're back in."

"Okay. You're the fashion guru." Ash didn't really care what was in. She pretty much wore whatever she felt like, without worrying about the current fashions, but tonight she wanted to get it right.

"Trust me. It'll be perfect."

"Thanks, Pen. I better go. I have to finish getting ready."

She hung up and tugged on the shirt, then pulled it back off, took off her bra, and pulled the top on again. She hoped he'd been serious when he said he didn't want her to wear a bra. She hated going without one, at least in public, because her breasts were large and needed the support. For him, she'd give it a try.

She started to put on the shorts, but hesitated, considering. Underwear or no underwear? She thought it might turn him on to know that she wasn't wearing anything at all under these clothes. Then again, he'd told her not to wear a bra, but said nothing about panties. If he was a Dom, and she wanted to impress him, maybe she should follow his instructions to the letter. Playing it safe might be better than showing initiative, this early in their relationship.

Still, maybe a thong? The shorts had loose legs, but were tight across the hips. Yes, a thong. No panty lines.

She finished dressing and went into the bathroom. She'd braided her hair earlier, after her shower. Now she put on a bit of eyeliner, light eye shadow and mascara, a touch of blush. Lip balm with just a hint of pale rose tint. She never wore foundation or powder because she hated the way it felt on her face. Plus, she liked a natural look.

She took a deep breath, appraising herself in the mirror. Ready as she'd ever be.

Oops, wait. She'd forgotten the belt. She returned to the bedroom and found the belt stuffed in her sock drawer. She shook it out and unkinked a couple of twisted links. After a moment's consideration, she tucked her shirt into her waistband and slipped the belt through the short's loops, hooking it so that a length of chain of about eight inches hung down.

She opened the closet door and checked herself in the full-length mirror. She had to admit Penny was right -- the outfit made her look good. The black shorts minimized her hips, the silver belt accentuating her waistline. The shirt, mostly black, minimized the extra weight she carried, but the clingy fabric and silver threads, glimmering as she moved, nicely accented the generous curves of her breasts.

The doorbell rang, and her heart skipped a beat. "Coming!"

She grabbed her purse from the dresser and hustled to the door.

"Hi!"

"Hi." Damon's gaze traveled from her head to her toes, resting just a tad longer on her chest than anywhere else. "Are you ready?"

"Mm-hmm." She stepped outside and turned to lock the door.

Damon stepped up behind her, his hands on her shoulders. He ducked his head, breathing in deep. "You smell good."

She could feel the heat of him against her back. "Thank you." Damn it, she was having trouble with the lock again. The fact that proximity to him was making her hand shake might have something to do with it.

"Let me." She could hear the smile in his tone, and her cheeks warmed as she handed him the keys. She didn't mind if he knew she liked him, but did she have to make such a fool of herself?

Of course, he had no problem with the lock. As they turned and headed for his car, he handed the keys back to her, grinning. "I missed you."

"Did you?"

He stopped and pulled her into his arms. His mouth ravaged hers, quick and hungry, tongue darting. Heat flushed her cheeks, her chest. She clung to him, knees trembling.

She was disappointed when he let go.

"What do you think?"

"I think you missed me," she answered in a small voice, still weak in the knees as they resumed their walk to the parking lot. He was the only man to ever make her weak with a kiss. "I thought…" She let her voice trail off.

He held the door to the Jeep open for her. "You thought…?" he prompted when she didn't finish her sentence.

She slid into the seat. "I…just hoped you hadn't forgotten."

Damon glanced around the parking lot. Catching her eye, he slid a hand up her inner thigh, beneath her shorts, toying with the curls that had escaped her tiny thong. "Did *you* forget?"

"No," she squeaked, hard-pressed to catch her breath.

"Then why would I?"

She shook her head, at a loss for words.

He slipped his hand out. Cupping her face with one hand, he brought his lips close to her ear. "I want you, Ash. Never doubt that."

"O-okay." Hot breath tickled her ear, and she trembled, pussy tingling.

"Do you want me?" His tongue traced the outer edge of her earlobe.

"Y-yes." God, if he asked her to fuck him, right here, right now, she'd probably do it. "Yes."

"I'm glad." His fingers trailed down her cheek, her neck. He lifted the edge of her low-cut collar, peeking inside. "Mmm. No bra." He settled the collar back into place, then cupped her breast, his thumb teasing her nipple through the thin fabric. "You remembered."

She nodded, suppressing a desperate whimper.

He watched her, moving his hand to the other breast, warming it with his palm, then pinching the nipple through her shirt. Warmth flooded her abdomen. The musky scent of her desire rose between them.

"Your eyes," he murmured. "They get darker when you're horny." He grinned. "I like that."

She nodded, keeping her eyes on his, knowing he liked that, wanting to give him everything he desired.

He let go and grabbed her shoulders, resting his forehead against hers. "We'd better go." He panted. "Or we'll never make it out of the parking lot."

Which would have been fine with *her*, but she nodded as he shut the door and went around to the driver's side.

He took her to a popular steakhouse for dinner. "I'm a meat-and-potatoes kind of guy," he said. "I hope that's not a problem."

"No way." Ash gestured toward her body. "I think it's obvious I like to eat. No tofu or veggie lasagna for me."

"Good. I can't stand to take a woman out to eat and watch her pick at a salad I paid six bucks extra for and finish only about a quarter of her meal." He let his eyes travel over her. "I think I prefer a woman with a little meat on her bones."

"You *think?*" she teased.

Seriously, he said, "To be honest, I usually date women a little less…" He looked panicked as he searched for a word.

She took pity on him. "Generous?"

Relief flooded his features. "Thank you, yes. Generous." His gaze swept over her again, his eyes hooded and sexy. Her pulse pounded in her ears, her nipples hardening. He noticed and grinned. "Yes. I definitely like generous. A lot."

She smiled back.

When the waitress came, he ordered the same thing for both of them. T-bones, medium, with loaded baked potatoes, no sour cream. "I should have asked. Do you like sour cream?" he said after the woman walked off.

"No, actually."

"I hope you didn't mind my ordering for you."

"Not at all." She looked him in the eye. "I like a man who knows what I want."

His dark-honey eyes smoldered. "Do something for me, Ash."

"Yes?"

"Play with your nipples. I want to be able to see them while we eat."

God. Her pussy flooded with juices. She leaned forward, crossing her arms and resting them on the table. While he watched, she subtly teased her nipples with the tips of her fingernails, bringing them to taut peaks beneath the form-hugging fabric.

"Nice," he breathed. Looking up, he tilted his head, indicating that the waitress was returning with their order.

After she was gone, Ash picked up her fork and flashed him a grin. Wiggling the utensil up and down between her thumb and forefinger, she let the edge of the handle just graze one black-and-silver-clad mound.

Damon breathed in sharply. "Keep them hard for me, Ash."

"Yes, Damon," she promised demurely.

The rest of the meal just about drove her crazy. She brushed her arms across her breasts reaching for salt and pepper, teased them with the handle ends of her fork and knife, let the edge of her iced-tea glass touch her nipples, condensation soaking into the fabric, cooling them, making them stand out even more. The more she touched them, the more the tension she sensed in Damon tightened.

They did manage some conversation. She found out he'd been in the Air Force for several years. That he'd been deployed to Iraq a few years earlier, and stayed for a year's tour. He'd been back in the States for three years, at Lackland for a little over one. He was an aircraft mechanic and loved his job, though he admitted that he had a tough time staying in the military. "I don't like taking orders. I can do it, but it's not a natural thing for me." He shrugged. "But I can't see myself working for a private airline. If I'm going to work on planes, I'd rather it be the ones that are helping to preserve our way of life."

Impressed, Ash nodded. No surprise that he didn't like taking orders, but she admired him for wanting to ply his trade in the place where it would do the most good. It had to be hard for someone like him, who wasn't an officer, to stay in the military when he was so obviously an alpha male.

Finally, the meal was over. Not that she hadn't enjoyed it, but she was about ready to explode, she was so horny. She kind of hoped Damon would nix the movie and turn back toward home.

But he still planned on seeing the movie, apparently, as he informed her on the way out of the restaurant. They were catching the newest Bruce Willis flick, which had actually been out a while, but she hadn't seen it yet, and she really liked Bruce -- though not nearly as much as she would have liked making love to Damon. Still, it wouldn't be a total loss, with Bruce to admire.

In the line outside the theater, Damon stood behind her. Wrapping his arms around her, he rested his chin on the top of her head. "I really enjoyed dinner."

"Me, too." Ash leaned into him, delighting in the sensation of his hard body pressed against hers.

His thumbs swept across her nipples, sending a shiver the length of her spine.

"Naughty boy," she whispered, tilting her head so she could see his face.

He raised his eyebrows. "Oh, I think you're much naughtier than I am." He studied her face. "Tell me you are, Ash."

She turned, wrapping her arms around his waist. "Is that what you want, Damon? A naughty girl?"

"Yes." His voice was thick with need, his cock hard against her tummy beneath his slacks.

"I'm anything you want me to be, Damon." She looked into his eyes, drowning in burnt amber. "Anything."

His lips covered hers, hard and hungry. She pressed into him, heart pounding, wanting to give him everything.

"Hey, you're up," a voice from behind him prompted.

They parted reluctantly, turning to the ticket window. Damon paid for their tickets. Ash licked slightly bruised lips while she waited, savoring their muted throbbing.

"Do you want popcorn or anything?" he asked as they entered the lobby.

"Oh, no. I'm stuffed."

He slid an arm around her waist, steering her toward the correct screen.

There was only one other couple and a group of three teenage boys in the theater, all sitting toward the front. Damon guided her to seats three rows from the back, all the way over. He took the seat next to the wall, and she sat beside him, his arm across her shoulders.

As the lights went down, his fingers fiddled with the edge of her collar. Ash smiled to herself, leaning to her right, resting her head against his chest. Not only was she very cozy, but he was able to slip his hand inside her shirt.

He followed the curve of her breast, rubbing his fingers lightly across her swollen nipple. Ash shivered. She'd played with them so much during dinner, they were ultra sensitive.

He reached over with his other hand, fooling with one fabric-covered nub while he caressed bare flesh with the other.

"Mmm." Ash slid a little lower in her seat, leaning into him a bit more.

Damon hooked the edge of her top with his forefingers and pulled it down to just below her nipples.

"Damon!"

"Shh." He licked the fingers of each hand, then stroked both her nipples into hard peaks.

"Mmmmm." She glanced around. They were still the only people in the back. The two groups up front were too far away to hear or see them. She looked at Damon. His eyes were riveted on her distended nipples, darting from one to the other. The dark summits glistened in the flickering light from the screen.

She arched her back, making her breasts stand out. Damon caught her nipples between the thumb and middle fingers of each hand, pinching.

"Oh!" Ash wriggled in her seat, keeping her voice low, but unable to keep from crying out. Her pussy throbbed, her clit tingling.

He wrapped his right hand around her left breast, the nipple still pinched tight between the fingers of his left hand. He lifted her breast, tugging it up, stretching the nipple. Ash moaned softly. "Suck it for me," he whispered.

Oh, God. She lowered her head, covering her stinging nipple with her hot mouth.

A spark of pleasure ignited in her abdomen. She moaned, muffled by the mouthful of flesh. Slowly, she began to suck.

A spasm rippled through her. Damn, it was *hot* to play with her body while he helped -- and watched. She sucked harder, trembling as warmth flooded her pussy.

"Yes," Damon breathed in her ear. He grabbed her right breast, pulling it up, pressing it to her mouth. "Now, both."

Ash covered them both, sucking. Her pussy throbbed. Even her ass tingled. Tiny wet sounds escaped where her lips failed to seal, and Damon shifted in his seat. "Oh, baby," he murmured softly. He took a deep breath. "I can smell you."

"Here." He let go and brought her hands up to support her breasts. She gripped them tight and even pulled them up a little more, so she could take more of each nipple into her mouth. Damon chuckled low and sexy. "So eager!"

He reached across and raised her left leg until her heel rested in her seat, opening her pussy to him. Then he slid his hand under the right leg of her shorts, pushing aside her curls, the narrow thong.

"Mm!" She was sucking hard and fast now, hips wriggling as short bursts of pleasure traveled from her nipples to her clit. When Damon's fingers pressed inside her, she almost screamed.

She raised her head, whispering urgently. "Yes!"

"Uh-uh," Damon protested. "Don't stop." He pressed her head back down to her breasts.

She sucked the peaks back into her mouth. His fingers plunged in and out of her weeping slit. She moaned again, nipping at the tips of her buzzing nubs.

A corkscrew of delight twisted through her pussy. She nibbled again, biting, sucking, the bliss winding tighter and tighter inside her. Oh, God. Oh! It was too much. She let her nipples go, tossing her head back.

She arched, hips thrusting, thrusting. She pressed her lips together to keep from screaming.

"That's it, Ash. Come!" His voice was thick, muted.

She froze, shudder after shudder rippling through her as her pussy spasmed repeatedly. She tossed her head back and forth, whimpering softly.

Damon brushed damp wisps of hair back from her temple. "Shh. Shh. It's all right," he whispered. "It's all right. Come down now."

And she was done. Just like that, even with his fingers still inside her, the orgasm passed.

Damn, he was good.

She collapsed into the seat, breathing heavily. Damon tugged his fingers free and grinned. While she watched, he licked each one, his eyes glinting gold as the flickering light from the screen caught them.

Taking a few deep breaths to calm herself, she sat up. She started to tug her neckline back into place, but Damon put a hand on hers. "Leave it."

She took another deep breath. Nodded. They settled into their seats, Damon's arm around her shoulder again. As they turned their attention to the movie -- having absolutely no idea now what was going on -- he toyed idly with her nipples.

Lord, he was going to be the death of her.

She forgot about the movie. Staring at the screen, she saw nothing, so focused was she on the sensations in her breasts. Her nipples stung, throbbed, ached, constantly stimulated by his touch.

By the time he tugged her top over her chest, about ten minutes before the film ended, she was nothing but a quivering heap of desire. Standing up to exit required an effort of will to keep her rubbery legs from buckling.

At the car, he drew her into his arms. "Did you enjoy the movie?"

She nodded, not trusting herself to speak.

He chuckled. "Horny?"

"Yes," she croaked.

"Good." He kissed her cheek, opened the door and helped her into the Jeep. "Let's go home."

As they reached the top of the stairs, Damon paused on the landing. After an instant's hesitation, he led Ash toward her door. Wordlessly, she handed him the keys. He smiled, smoothly opening the door and stepping aside as she entered.

He went in and shut the door behind him, throwing the deadbolt.

Before she knew it, he had picked her up and perched her on the table beneath the mirror. She let her purse slide off her shoulder to the floor. He tugged her collar down, exposing both breasts.

He bent, mouth closing on one engorged nipple. Ash gasped, running her fingers through his blond hair. "Oh, Damon. Yes," she whispered.

His hands crept to her waist. After a moment of fumbling, he managed to unfasten her silver link belt. He eased it from the loops.

Releasing her breast, he wrapped the belt around her chest, positioning two of the links so that they perfectly framed her nipples. "Oh!"

Crossing the ends around her back, he tugged, pulling the belt tight so that her nipple and a mouthful of areola puckered from the center of each link.

He bent his head again, tracing the outline of each oval with his tongue. Ash moaned, hands clenching on his shoulders. He pulled the chain tighter, pressing the links into her chest. "Yes," Ash whispered, wrapping her legs around his waist.

Groaning, he sucked one raw nipple into his mouth. She arched, running her fingers through his prickly hair. The short buzz tickled her hands.

Damon sucked harder. Ash gasped, pressing into him. The chain tightened a little more. "Oh, yes," she moaned, wriggling against him.

He switched sides, sucking the other tender peak into his mouth, catching the tip between his teeth. "Oh, God." He nipped her gently. "Oh!" Ash thrust her hips. The chain tightened around her. Damon nibbled again.

"Oh, God, Damon." Ash panted, prickles of sweet agony cascading from her nipple to her pussy. She clutched his shoulders. He sucked her in, taking as much of her areola into his mouth as the link allowed, and bit down. Not hard enough to break the skin, but hard enough to make her release a short, thrilled scream. Arching, she ground against him.

He dropped the chain, stepping back with a look of horror on his face. "No-no-no," she moaned. She scooted off the table, unfastening her shorts, pushing them down. "Please, Damon. I liked it. I need it."

He shook his head, but she saw his fists clench, hands trembling. He was holding back again, trying to save her from…what?

"Damon." She reached out and started unbuckling his belt. He grabbed her hands.

"I can't."

She stared up at him in disbelief.

His face pale, covered with a fine sheen of sweat, he gently pushed her hands away and stepped back. "I'm sorry, Ash." He felt for the doorknob behind him. "I have to go."

"Damon, I --"

He turned and flipped the deadbolt, striding out before she could stop him. She went to the doorway, watching in stunned silence as he crossed the landing, unlocked his door, and stepped inside without a backward glance.

Chapter Eight: Cut and Run

Damon leaned, trembling, against the inside of the front door. He ran shaky fingers over his face, his scalp, then stared at his hands.

He felt the chain again, chill silver against his palms. He'd wanted to wrap them around her twice, three times. Pull and keep on pulling, tormenting her darkening nipples with his tongue until she begged him for release.

But he'd held back. He'd paced himself, tightening it only a little, a couple of times, convincing himself he might be able to make it through the night without hurting her. Just the mildest bit of bondage play, nothing that would really cause her pain.

But her breast in his mouth -- she'd tasted so good. He had to bite.

His cock tingled at the memory. Her tender flesh trapped between his teeth, her response, grinding against him.

But the *scream*. He shuddered. Images of war-torn bodies in Iraq -- men and women wailing in pain -- had flooded him at the sound.

He slid down the door to sit on the floor, head in his hands. He'd almost fucked her. Lord knew he'd wanted to. His cock still throbbed, swollen and aching.

But the images reminded him. Causing pain was wrong. He owed those injured -- soldiers, innocent bystanders, all of them -- some deference. Their pain had to be respected. He wouldn't cause harm in the pursuit of pleasure and demean the sacrifices they'd made for the sake of their countries.

He shook his head, wincing when it pounded. The migraine was starting. Memories were flickering at the edges of his awareness, demanding he acknowledge them.

Well, at least now he knew. The decision was made. He couldn't see her anymore. She was too perfect, too right for him. There was no way he could be with Ash and not want it all, *not* want to take her in the way that was natural.

Natural -- at least for *him* -- but not right. Not anymore.

Moaning, he pushed up from the floor, then staggered into the bathroom and downed two of his pills. With his head pounding like an anvil, he turned on the shower, stepping inside before the water even warmed.

His cock throbbed painfully. Groaning, he wrapped his hand around it. Propping himself up against the wall with the other, he stroked up and down, fast.

Faster, until his skin stung.

It wouldn't work. He slapped the wall in frustration, body aching all over, dizzy from the pain in his head. Abruptly, he turned the water off. Stepping out of the shower, he didn't even bother drying. He went into the bedroom and collapsed on top of the quilt, the ceiling fan making him shiver as it dried his wet skin.

No more Ash.

He wished he could somehow make it up to her -- it wasn't her fault; it was him -- but nothing he could do or say would change things. He had to stay away from her. He couldn't control himself when he was with Ash, and the person he became was someone he needed to keep buried, for his own peace of mind.

He moaned. The faint sound of chopper blades and muted wails echoed in his ears.

Please, God, let sleep take me before the phantoms come.

Ash closed the door after Damon disappeared behind his, shivering despite the night's warmth. She picked up her shorts and wandered into the living room in a daze.

What the hell went wrong?

She sat on the couch, twisting the garment in her hands. It had been a magical night, sultry and sensual, full of sexual promise...even good conversation, over dinner.

Then Damon went nuts. She'd never forget his expression. Horrified. Like he suddenly couldn't stand the sight of her.

But he'd still wanted her. He hadn't gone limp like the last time. She'd felt his cock, rigid and ready, when she was unfastening his belt. And she was sure he'd wanted to finish the job. She'd seen it in his clenched hands, the trembling muscles, once again gaining the impression that a leashed beast lived just below his surface, straining to break free.

She curled up on her side, resting her head on a throw cushion. Hot tears streaked her cheeks. Stupid to cry. They barely knew each other. She hadn't lost a thing.

The words didn't ring true. Not in her heart. He wanted her. He *needed* her, and she needed him.

So why was he fighting it?

She sniffed. Didn't really matter, did it? She wasn't about to approach him again, not after tonight. And hopefully he'd stay away from her as well. She sure as hell couldn't face an apology, even if he felt inclined to offer one. *That* would be more humiliating than the actual incident. "*Sorry I couldn't sleep with you the other night, Ash, but I suddenly realized who I was with, and the idea was so horrifying...*"

She shook her head. She knew deep down inside that wasn't the problem. There was something else, something he didn't want to talk about. Maybe she'd been right to think there'd been some sort of accident with a sub.

Still, he hadn't confided in her, and now he wouldn't get the chance. If there was one thing she'd learned over the years, it was how to cut her losses. Damon Wayland was out of her life.

For good.

Chapter Nine: Frustration is Hell

The past few weeks had been a living hell.

Damon swore at a stubborn nut on the F-16 engine he was troubleshooting. *Frigging cheap parts.* He grabbed another wrench and pounded at the handle of the one he was trying to turn.

The nut came off, along with half the bolt.

"Damn!" He slammed his tools to the ground and kicked at the tarmac.

"Staff Sergeant Wayland."

He straightened, nodding to his superior. Master Sergeant Grey nodded. "In my office, Wayland. Now."

Shit. Whatever this was, it couldn't be good. He rolled his head, working the kinks out of his neck as he followed the master sergeant across the pitch.

"Take a seat." MSgt. Grey waved at a chair in front of his desk and shut the door. Damon sat on the edge of the seat and waited, back ramrod straight, while the man moved behind his desk. The sergeant's worn leather chair creaked as he lowered himself into it.

"You've been having some problems, Wayland."

No use denying it. He'd only be postponing the inevitable. "Yes, sir."

"I've had complaints about lack of cooperation, fits of temper..." Grey raised his eyebrows, apparently waiting for some kind of response.

Damon didn't know what to say, except, "Yes, sir."

His superior's eyes narrowed. "You're my best mechanic, Wayland."

"Yes, sir."

"The only thing saving your ass right now is the respect your coworkers and I have for those abilities." He tapped a pen against the desk. "No one likes you, Wayland. You're surly, uncommunicative, and disrespectful. I made some calls, and from what I've heard, these problems started in Iraq and they've only gotten worse."

Grey stood and paced in front of the window that looked out into the aircraft bay. "If I'd received any formal, written complaints, Wayland, you'd be in serious trouble." He turned and regarded Damon sternly. "As it is, I'm going to ask you a question."

"Yes, sir." Damon took a deep breath, not sure what was coming.

"Do you want counseling?"

Damon started. Counseling? He sure as hell hadn't expected *that*. "No, sir. Why would I need counseling, sir?"

Grey sighed. "I don't know, Wayland. That's *your* business. What I do know is, I'm giving you exactly one month to figure out how to fit in here. If you don't work it out on your own, I'll *order* your ass to the shrink. Got that?"

Damon stood, nodding smartly. "Yes, sir!" He turned to go.

"You haven't been dismissed."

Damon froze in the act of reaching for the door handle and turned back, arms pressed to his sides, at attention. "Sorry, sir!"

The sergeant regarded him for a moment. "Look. Like I said, you're the best. That's why I'm willing to give you a chance to get right on your own. But in the meantime -- and it pains me to say this -- you're on inventory duty. I don't want you working on my planes until I'm certain your head's straight."

Damon closed his eyes for a split second. Crap. That wouldn't help; it would make things harder. He'd be pissed off *and* bored out of his skull. Unfortunately, there wasn't a damn thing he could do about it. He sighed, forcing back a protest. "Yes, sir!"

Grey sighed. "Take your tools and roster to Parker. Then report to Mitchell."

"Yes, sir."

"One month, Wayland."

"I understand, sir."

"Dismissed."

Damon nodded again and turned, then opened the door and marched smartly out to the plane. He grabbed his tools and replaced them in his kit, then rolled it across the airfield, heading for Parker, his mind racing.

Damon tossed his coveralls onto the bed and stepped into the bathroom for a quick shower. He came out rubbing his short stubble with a towel. He opened a drawer and pulled out underwear and a pair of jogging shorts and tugged them on.

He padded into the kitchen and threw together a ham and turkey sandwich, then grabbed a bottle of water and a bag of chips and carried them all out to his back porch.

The yards for the townhomes weren't that wide, but they were deep, and the woman who'd lived here before him had kept a nice garden.

But no, Ash had said the lady wasn't much of a gardener. Maybe the people before that, then.

It wasn't a bad place to sit and think. He wondered if Ash had been in the habit of watering and weeding back here, too. Before *he* came. He'd managed to water it enough that it hadn't died. Yet.

He sighed, setting his food on the rough wooden picnic table he'd picked up at a garage sale, something he'd spotted one weekend during his morning jog. The day had started out bad and gotten worse. There couldn't be anything duller than counting washers and screws. He'd spent the afternoon simmering in resentment, though he knew it was unjustified. He *had* been a prick lately. Even more so than usual, since the incident with Ash.

He settled onto the bench. Laughter sounded from next door, and he glanced over the fence.

His backyard was terraced, and the porch he sat on was high enough that he could easily see into Ash's yard. Near the back of hers, she'd set up a volleyball net, and she and a few friends were bopping a ball back and forth.

She looked better than she'd seemed the last few times he'd seen her. A couple of days after their date, he'd run into her coming home from work as he was leaving to grab a bite to eat. She'd already seemed pale to him, and as he stood aside for her to pass on the stairway, she whitened even further. She practically ran the last few steps. He could hear her fumbling with the lock, and turned away, hurrying down the steps, knowing she would be embarrassed if she knew he'd noticed.

And that's how it went. Whenever they happened to be outside at the same time, they ignored each other completely. She still watered his front flowerbed, but she managed to do it when he wasn't around. He halfway suspected she might be coming home from work to do it during the day, just so she knew there wouldn't be any chance of running into him.

He would have taken over, but he couldn't bring himself to go next door and tell her she didn't have to do it anymore.

He'd hated seeing her so pale and withdrawn. Previously so bold and full of life, she was like a ghost now, flitting around the edges of his senses.

Right now, jumping around on the lawn, she had a bit of color in her cheeks. As he watched, she dove for the ball and missed, coming up laughing.

God. He wished he could make her laugh. Hell, he'd settle for a smile. A nod, even. Anything would be better than this blind, painful silence between them.

He jerked his attention back to the table. Tearing open his potato chips, he forced himself to eat.

He had to figure out what to do. Nearly everything set him off nowadays, from the way people looked at him to the way the creases in his pants fell. Hell, maybe he *did* need a shrink.

He'd never talked to anyone about what had happened in Iraq. Even though he hadn't been in the line of fire, he'd been exposed to the results of the war nearly every day. Though he was a mechanic, he'd been pressed into service often to help the wounded and dying onto air transports. When he saw all that pain, he couldn't help but question his lifestyle. As time had passed, it became harder and harder to justify to himself the idea of hurting someone for pleasure. It seemed like a betrayal of the men and women who fought and died for his country.

But he was starting to realize that for him, the BDSM had been an important outlet. He'd chosen to go into the military as an enlisted man, knowing he was an alpha, knowing he wasn't well suited to taking orders. The tension of reining in his true nature every day had been alleviated by the D/s weekends.

But how could he go back to that? He kept coming up against this wall inside himself, plastered with the faces of the wounded and painted with bright neon letters: *Pain is wrong. Pain is bad. How can you enjoy inflicting it?*

Only in Iraq had he ever felt compelled to question his choice. Only there had he suddenly decided there was something wrong with him.

He didn't know what he'd do if he ended up kicked out of the Air Force. As much as he hated not being in charge, he loved working with aircraft, and he loved knowing that he was doing something for his country. Plus, he loved the small planes, the fighters, the drones. He couldn't give that up.

Wouldn't.

He glanced toward Ash's again and caught her gazing up at him. She averted her eyes immediately.

His heart skipped a beat. He would have expected anger or accusation, but she just looked...sad.

What if...*nah.* He picked up his sandwich and took a couple of bites, carefully keeping his concentration on the meal before him and off of the neighbor's backyard.

But now that the thought had occurred to him, he couldn't ignore it. Ash still cared for him. If she didn't, she'd be angry, not upset. During their short acquaintance, he'd been able to joke with her, laugh -- things he hadn't been able to do with anyone for quite some time. She seemed to understand him instinctively, just as he'd sensed certain things about her from the very beginning.

Could he talk to her? Could he tell her about his past -- *everything* about his past? If she understood what was happening with him, maybe they could work through it. Maybe they could find a way to be together and be happy.

He wasn't sure. If they tried again and it didn't work out, he didn't know if he could take that.

He'd have to think about it, and think hard.

Because he had a feeling that whatever was wrong in his life, he might not be able to fix it without her.

Chapter Ten: Whispers in the Dark

She was getting up at three in the morning to water his plants.

He'd been trying to catch her alone for a couple of days. He made sure he was outside when she came home in the evening, but the first day, Penny had come driving up right behind her, so he'd walked on past and gone out to dinner even though he hadn't been planning to. The next day, she didn't show up at her regular time. He finally ended up going back inside and didn't hear her key in her lock until after nine.

Tonight, he'd lain awake, unable to sleep until well past midnight. He finally got up and went into the kitchen, snacking on cheese and pickles while he watched an old Clint Eastwood flick on The Movie Channel.

At three o'clock, he heard a door open and shut. He flipped up a slat in the blinds he'd finally hung in the front window and saw Ashland walking down the stairs. In a moment, he heard pipes squeal briefly as she turned on the water.

She watered her own plants first, then dragged the hose across the sidewalk and tackled his.

He let the slat fall. Okay, so…there she was. This was his opportunity.

He set his plate down and stood up. He took a deep breath, then opened the front door and stepped out onto the landing.

He took the steps down two by two, then sat on the bottom one, watching her.

He knew she'd seen him. Her body stiffened, and she stopped moving the hose from side to side. He decided he'd wait until she acknowledged him.

After a while, she wrapped the arm not holding the hose around her middle as though she were cold.

The trickle of liquid that had made a path out to the sidewalk turned into a stream.

He waited a little longer, then said, "I think you're drowning them."

Her hand shook as she turned around slowly, finally facing him.

"I'll turn it off," he said. He stood up and went over to the faucet. The knob squeaked as he rotated it. When he was done, he wiped his damp palm on his boxers.

Ash stood beside the sidewalk, still holding the hose. He took it from her and wrapped it up, setting the coils on the small cement square beneath the faucet. Then he sat down again on the bottom step.

The streetlamp and moonlight combined to make the night fairly bright. He saw her close her eyes and give a little shake of her head. Then she walked over and sat down beside him.

"What do you want, Damon?" she asked after a short silence.

"You."

She didn't answer right away. They sat together listening to the crickets.

She finally turned to face him, her brow furrowed. "I don't know if I'm up to that, Damon." She looked down at her hands, clasped together in her lap. "I...I told myself you were out of my life for good."

He picked up a leaf and twirled it this way and that between his fingers, just to give his hands something to do. "Is that what you *really* want?"

She glanced at him. "I think...I *thought*...I don't know. It doesn't seem right to say this so soon, especially after what's happened, but I thought maybe you were...the one. The person I could maybe..." Her voice trailed away, and she looked down at her hands again.

Love? he guessed, knowing he was right. She sounded apprehensive, but...hopeful. Relief flooded him. *Yes.* She still wanted to try and work things out.

He closed his eyes, overwhelmed for a moment. When he opened them, he reached out and clasped her hands in his.

Her body stiffened, but she didn't pull away.

"Look at me, Ash."

She hesitated, but finally raised her eyes to his.

"I feel the same way."

Her mouth turned down. "I don't understand, Damon. You...you run hot and cold. One minute, I think possibly you're going to be the love of my life; the next, it's like I'm the Bride of Frankenstein, and you're running in the opposite direction." She looked at his hands covering hers, and Damon's throat tightened as a tear slid down the curve of her moon-kissed cheek. "I know you probably don't want to hear this, but I care for you too much to play games. I think I might be in love with you. If you're not looking for the same thing, then --" Her voice broke on a soft sob.

"I am." He leaned forward, catching her face between his hands, making her look at him. "I *am*, Ash."

She tried to shake her head, but he held her fast.

"Ash. I know you're scared. I never meant for things to happen the way they did. You have to believe me."

"Damon, I just --"

He knew it wasn't fair, but he kissed her. Tenderly. The barest brush of his lips against hers. She smelled of honeysuckle and new-mown grass and second chances, and he prayed, as his lips hovered near hers, not quite touching them now, that she wanted them to be together as much as he did.

She faltered just long enough that he thought the answer would be no, but then her lips touched his. Trembling, cautious, like a butterfly resting briefly on a flower.

"Come here," he whispered. He pulled her onto his lap, so that she straddled him.

Her eyes were closed, and he caressed her cheek with the back of his hand. "Look at me, Ash."

She shook her head.

"Please."

She smiled through tears. "I'm afraid if I open my eyes, this will all be a dream."

He wiped the tears away. "Ash. Look at me." He spoke quietly, but with a definite tone of command.

She opened her eyes.

He slid his hands up under her top and around her waist. She wore a spaghetti-strap baby doll of silky material, and loose-fitting shorts that matched. While he looked into her eyes, he slipped his hands under her waistband.

His pulse beat a quick tattoo. No panties.

Ash's breathing quickened as he caressed the mounds of her buttocks, the curve of her hips. He brought one hand around, diving down into her thick bush, finding her clit.

Her cheeks flushed as he played with the nub, her brown eyes flashing bronze in the street light.

With his free hand, he tucked his boxers down, exposing his swollen cock.

Ash tilted her head to look, but he caught her chin and brought it back up.

Eyes riveted to hers, he grasped her waist, urging her up onto her knees, resting to either side of his hips on the riser.

He held her shorts aside and guided her down onto his cock.

The touching of her slick lips to his engorged head made him shiver. "Ash," he whispered in a voice hoarse with need.

She lowered herself slowly, easing him inside her, gasping when his thickness stretched her lips taut.

He offered, though he thought it might kill him if she accepted, "If we need to wait --"

She hesitated for just a moment.

"I'm disease-free, Ash," he whispered in her ear. "Tested six months ago, even though I hadn't been with anyone in a year, and no one since."

Even in the muted light, he saw her cheeks redden. "I stayed on the pill, even though...and I was disease-free the last time I was tested, but that's been a couple of years ago because..." She looked away, as though embarrassed. "Well, there hasn't been anyone."

God, he wanted her so bad. But not if she had any doubts whatsoever. "It's up to you, baby. We can wait, if you want."

Ash shook her head, her eyes meeting his, bright and eager as she worked her way onto his shaft.

Wet and warm, her pussy surrounded him. He groaned. It had been so long.

"Ash," he growled urgently. Her eyes widened when she saw his expression. He could only imagine what his gaze might be revealing -- the desperation, the desire.

She gripped his shoulders, pressing herself down around him. "God, Ash."

She leaned forward, still looking him in the eye, and whispered, "Help me." Her hot breath kissed his lips.

His hands spasmed, tightening on her waist. He thrust, hard and deep. Ash took in a sharp breath, stiffening.

"Are you all --"

"Don't stop," she panted, her eyes dark and glazed with need.

That's all it took. His hands held her still as he drove himself deeper. "Yes," she breathed. "Oh, Damon, yes."

He drew back, then slammed into her again.

"Yes!"

He couldn't slow, couldn't stop. Now that he was finally inside her, he had to mark her, had to claim her. Had to make her *his*. He lunged, burying his entire length in her delicious warmth.

"Mmmm, yes."

And again.

"Oh, God. Yes. Yes!" Her hands tightened on his shoulders, nails digging into his back. He gasped, his cock throbbing. A ball of fire expanded in his groin, and he held his breath, watching her eyes go unfocused, feeling his cock spasm as her pussy tightened around him.

His seed spilled, bathing them both in warmth. Ash's pussy sucked at him. Her breath came in short gasps.

Heat raced through his veins, tingling in his fingers, his toes. He arched, a sensation of pleasure so intense that he couldn't find a name for it ripping through his cock.

"Oh!" Ash's eyes widened. Her pussy contracted again and again. She gasped, staring into his eyes, shuddering in unison with him. *Oh, yes. They were MADE for each other.*

After an eternity of bliss, they both came down from their high. Damon collapsed against the uncomfortable stone steps, knowing they'd both probably have bruises in the morning. Ash rested against him, her head on his chest.

"Mmmm." She ran her fingers lightly over his shoulder and down along his arm. "Finally."

He chuckled. "Yeah." He frowned slightly. "Too quick, though."

She raised her head to look at him. "See? That wasn't so bad."

His smile faded. "Ash, we still need to talk. There are some things you need to know about me."

She nodded. "All right." Then she pressed a finger to his lips when he started to speak again. "But not tonight. Tonight, I want you to come to bed with me."

He started to protest, but she cut him off again. "Just hold me," she said. "Just... *be* there."

Could he handle spending the night in a bed with her?

It didn't really matter. At this point, any hesitation on his part might break the fragile trust Ash had just offered him again. "Yes," he said.

She stood and held out a hand. Damon rose and wrapped her hand in his, following her up the stairs and through the front door.

Chapter Eleven: A History of the War

Damon winced. Bright sunlight streamed through the window, warming his face. What the hell happened to his blackout shades?

His arm rested on something warm and yielding. As he shifted, he heard a sigh, felt a thick braid moving against his chest.

Oh. Yeah.

He sat up in the bed, cracking his eyelids open just a hair, taking a moment to adjust to the brilliant illumination.

Ash rolled onto her back beside him. "Damon?"

He forced his eyes fully open. "Good morning," he mumbled.

Her features were blank as she studied him for a long moment. He tilted his head and smiled down at her.

Reassured, her face brightened, her lips curving into a grin. "It is, isn't it?"

He nodded, running his fingers lightly down her arm.

She shivered. "Thank you."

"For being an ass?" Frowning, he shook his head. "Don't thank me. I don't deserve it."

"You're wrong." She shifted the pillows, propping herself up in the bed beside him. "It was over. Chance meetings were awkward, but we would have gotten over that. Eventually, we would have been strangers again. That would have been the easy way to go, in the long run." She reached out, her fingernails lightly tracing his jaw line. "I'm so glad you didn't pick the easy way."

"Don't make me sound like a saint. I'm not."

"I know." She frowned. "I keep wondering if you're worried because…" She shook her head and sighed. "Look, I -- I recognized the pins on that towel. I know Original Sin. I've been there, as a sub."

He shifted so that he was sitting toward the middle of the bed, staring at her. "What?"

"The stuff that fell out of that box the day you moved in. I didn't pay attention to the rest, but that towel I tossed you? I recognized some of the lapel pins, or whatever they're called. NCSF, Sexual Independence Now, I know those organizations. I belong to SIN. And I went to the club, Original Sin, when I visited a friend in San Francisco."

Wow. That explained a lot, like why he'd felt she was a natural sub, why they'd been so drawn to each other. She'd been sending him signals all along. He didn't know whether to be pleased or angry.

His long silence obviously unnerved her. "Damon?"

"I'm…very surprised." He ran a hand through his bristly hair. "This might make things more difficult."

"Difficult? But why? I thought it would be a good thing."

He shook his head. "I'm having...problems with that aspect of my nature."

"Oh." Her eyes widened as understanding dawned. "Oh! Is that what --"

"Yes."

"Do you want to talk about it?"

"We have to."

"Okay. Um, now?"

He glanced down, taking in his boxers. "Why don't I go change? It might be a good idea to talk about this somewhere...not so private." He grinned. "Since we have a hard time keeping our hands off each other, and this is important. We need to get through this discussion before we can move forward."

She nodded. "All right."

"When I get back, I'll take you to breakfast."

"I'll be ready."

Unlike the last time, Damon kept the conversation generic during their meal. After they'd finished eating, he refilled their coffees and sat back.

Ash straightened in her seat, as though sensing that he was about to get down to business.

"I've known I was a Dom since I was in high school," he said. "I sort of stumbled into it, but once I realized how much I liked it, I was hooked." He took a sip of coffee. "I read a lot of books, found a really good mentor who taught me a lot, and eventually I joined a couple of groups and started seriously playing.

"I wasn't ready for long-term relationships. I played at parties, and did short-term contracts."

Ash shifted in her seat.

"Did you want to say something?" he asked.

"I just wondered...how heavily were you into it? I mean, how often?"

"Heavily. Every weekend, once I graduated high school and was on my own. Not quite as often once I joined the Air Force, but as often as I could." He took a deep breath and leaned forward. "Then I was sent to Iraq. As an aircraft mechanic, I wasn't in the line of fire, but I saw things. People hurt, maimed. I was okay for a while, but after about six months, I just...I couldn't justify, to myself, the pleasure that I got from inflicting pain. Of course, that's not the only aspect of the lifestyle, but it's one of the things I enjoyed most as a Dom.

"I'd found a couple of people at Balad that were into D/s, and we'd played a couple of times, but all of the sudden, it became hard. I'd be in the middle of a scene, and I'd hear the screams of the wounded, instead of the sub. I started seeing the faces of people I'd helped load onto airlifts, people who were injured too badly to be treated, even there, and...I quit."

Ash regarded him with compassion. "I understand, Damon. If...if we have to keep BDSM out of our --"

"That's the problem." He sighed, catching her eyes with his. "I've never believed in love at first sight, and I'm still kind of reluctant to say this is love, but I've never felt about anyone the way I feel about you. It's as if you were made for me. I was preoccupied the day I moved in, but the next day, through the window, when I stopped to really look at you, there was an instant attraction. Whenever I'm around you, the Master in me wants to come *out*."

"I see." Ash cupped her coffee mug with her hands. "So, where do we go from here?"

He ran a hand over his buzz cut. "I don't know. Last night worked, but I think that had to do with the fact that we were outside, where someone might see us -- the Dom tendency's always easier to control when I'm in a public place. And, well, I was desperate not to scare you off again. If we're seeing each other on a regular basis, spending time alone..."

"You might not be able to stop yourself," she finished.

He nodded.

Her brow furrowed. "Would that really be so bad? I mean, are you so sure you want to give up the lifestyle?"

He spread his hands. "You tell me. When the urge to dominate gets strong, I start hearing and seeing those faces. I get migraines. I have times like that first morning, when I can't" -- they were speaking softly, but he looked around to make sure no one was near them -- "perform."

"Have you talked to anyone about this?"

He shook his head. "I thought I was handling it okay. I told my doctor about the images of the wounded and the migraines, and he gave me some medication for the headaches, but I didn't tell him everything.

"And now, well, now the dam seems to be about to break. I've been getting more and more irritable. I'm in trouble at work..." He rubbed his forehead. "I have to find a way to deal with this, once and for all."

Ash took a deep breath and leaned forward. "Maybe you should stop trying to be something you're not."

He snapped his head up. "That's not what I was suggesting."

"I know." She sighed. "Look, I'm not a shrink. If you want a professional opinion, you should *see* a professional. But the things you do with your sexual or life partner, that's personal. It doesn't have anything to do with what went on in Iraq."

"But I just keep thinking. About how those people were willing to give so much for their country, and what was done to them in return. How can I justify inflicting pain just so I can get off?" His tone was rough.

"Damon. There's more to BDSM than that. Being a Master is about giving your partner what they need. It's consensual. Masters never inflict more pain than their sub can handle.

"You're an alpha male. A strong Dominant. I knew that the moment we met. You've submerged your alpha nature at work, and now you're...brainwashing yourself into giving up something that's integral to you in your private life, as well. It has to be hard for someone like you to stay in the military, especially when you're not an officer, and now you've cut off your only other outlet. Did you get into trouble at work because *we* weren't seeing each other, or because you never give yourself a chance to *be* yourself?"

She was making sense, but he frowned. "What about the visions, Ash? The headaches."

"I'm not sure." She stared into her coffee cup, as though searching for inspiration, then looked up. "Maybe if we start slow." She hesitated, then looked him in the eye. "I'll be honest. In public life, I'm a businesswoman. I'm making decisions, telling people what to do, controlling every aspect of the lab every day. Like you, I'm submerging my true nature, in order to be able to function at work.

"I *need* to be able to leave that behind when I come home. I've been looking for the right Dom for so long, I'd pretty much given up. I think *you're* the guy." She looked apologetic. "A minute ago, I started to say that if we had to keep BDSM out of our lives, I could deal with it. But I realize…I don't think I could. I'd always *know*, deep down inside, what you were. I'd never stop wanting that. In the end, we could go from not having a relationship at all to having one where *I'm* resenting you because you can't be what I need, and *you're* resenting me for wanting that."

She swallowed hard, and tears sprang to her eyes. "I think what I'm trying to say is, I'd rather have nothing than have something that's not truly right for you *or* for me."

Damon couldn't quite process what she was saying. He leaned back in the booth, stunned.

"I know that sounds selfish, or like I don't care, but I *do*. That's why it has to be right, Damon. There's so much potential here. If we don't explore it, we'll be living a half-life." Her eyes begged him to understand. "I want this to last, Damon, so much. I don't know how to tell you how much. But only if it's the real thing. And it can't be real if you're not being *you*."

Damon closed his eyes. He wanted so much to give in, to say, "Okay, I'll be me again." But the visions and migraines had started *before* he gave up BDSM; they weren't a *result* of giving it up. If they tried, and it didn't work…"I don't know, Ash. I need to think about this."

"All right, Damon." Her eyes were still full of tears, but she managed a smile. "I'll wait."

Chapter Twelve: Lighting the Candle

Damon paced back and forth in his living room. It had been a week since he'd spoken with Ash, a week where he'd made his decision a hundred times and then changed his mind. She was probably right about everything, but he'd spent three and a half years convincing himself that he had to give up the kinky side of his nature, and he was having a hard time coming to terms with the idea that all the frustration, the isolation, had been a waste.

But things *had* been getting steadily worse for him. He used to make an effort to know the people he worked with. He'd been easygoing, well liked. Uncorking the Master so often on the weekends must have had a lot to do with that sense of contentment, because he couldn't remember being this miserable since before he'd discovered BDSM.

Why was he putting off the inevitable? He had to go back to being himself, before his whole life came crashing down around him.

But he knew why. He stopped pacing, staring at his faint reflection in the glass covering the painting that hung in his living room. He'd waited so long. He was afraid. Afraid he'd get carried away once he started again. Afraid he'd lose his control.

Afraid he'd hurt Ash.

His computer dinged. He'd forgotten he'd brought up his e-mail account earlier. He walked over and moved the mouse, the screensaver disappearing.

Hey, Damon! It's been great hearing from all my old friends the last couple of weeks. I've been talking to the other guys, and if we can all manage it, we'd like to try getting the old gang together again in person. We're thinking about meeting in November. Since we're all scattered, some of us might have to travel. Let me know if you're interested.

He'd finally managed to find one of his high school buddies via the Internet. Through that, old phone numbers, and parents who had kept in touch, they'd managed to locate the other two, and he and the gang had renewed their friendship. He typed quickly: *Definitely. Just let me know the time and place; I'll be there. Traveling is no problem*, and hit Send.

He sat in the overstuffed recliner across from the television. It would be good to see his old buddies again. He'd been happy in high school, unlike a lot of people. One reason for that was because he'd had friends that knew exactly who and what he was, and accepted him for it.

Which brought him back to...He sat up and grabbed the phone. Ash had given him her number when he brought her back home after their discussion, and he'd memorized it that same day. He punched the numbers and waited.

"Hello?"

"Ash?" He took a deep, steadying breath. "I'd like you to come over tonight. I have a surprise for you."

He had everything ready before the doorbell rang. Looking the spare bedroom over one last time, he nodded and shut the door.

He headed down the hall and through the living room and opened the front door. "Ash."

She looked uncertain, a little apprehensive. "Hi, Damon."

"Come in."

She stepped inside and glanced around quickly.

"Have a seat." Damon gestured at the couch.

She lowered herself onto the sofa, scooting into the corner. He sat down and faced her. "I want to give it a try."

She closed her eyes. Her hands, where they clutched her purse, trembled.

"Ash?"

She swallowed and looked up. "I wasn't sure what to expect. I'm just...very relieved."

He reached out and gently confiscated her purse, setting it off to one side. "I know. I'm sorry for making you wait, but I had to think."

"It's okay."

He shook his head. "No, but I'm hoping to make it up to you." He smiled. "We haven't talked about limits or preferences. I...I don't know if I can do that tonight. If we talk about some things...well, it would probably be better to wait until I've let off some steam."

"I understand."

He leaned forward, excited and a little anxious. "I know it's advanced, but wax play is about sensuality with me, not pain. I'm very experienced -- it's one of my specialties. It's a scene I think I'll be comfortable in, this first time out. If that's --"

"Yes," Ash breathed.

"Are you sure?"

"I trust you, Damon."

Holy shit. Though he'd prepared optimistically, he hadn't been sure she'd agree to such serious play this first time out. He took a deep breath. This woman was absolutely perfect for him. He'd better not fuck this up. "Okay. Then, if you'll undress, I'll get some ice."

Ash stood and shimmied out of her skirt and blouse. She was wearing a bra and panties. She noticed his quick frown and caught his eye. "I wasn't sure...you didn't say."

He nodded. "That's fine. I wanted to surprise you. But" -- he stepped close and unfastened her bra -- "from now on, I'll tell you what to wear when we're together." He tossed the bra aside as she stepped out of her underwear. "*Exactly* what to wear."

"Yes, Damon."

She waited quietly while he filled a champagne bucket with ice; then she followed him down the hall into the spare bedroom.

He had covered the bed with a transparent, unadorned shower curtain. On the bedside table were several fat, white paraffin candles, a lighter, an eye mask, two basting brushes, a small artist's paintbrush, and a slow cooker in which additional paraffin wax already melted, a food thermometer attached to the side so that he could regulate the temperature.

On a TV tray next to the bed, he'd placed shaving cream, a washcloth, a woman's razor, and a bowl.

He turned to Ash. "I planned on shaving you before the wax play. It will make removing the wax easier." He shrugged. "And I'd just really enjoy doing it."

She nodded. Now that they were actually moving things along, she seemed to have lost her tongue.

"Ash, are you sure about this?"

She looked up from the paraphernalia on the table. "What? Yes! I just...I'm having trouble believing it's finally happening."

He wrapped his arms around her. "I couldn't give you up, Ash."

She hugged him back. After several seconds, he stepped back. "I'll go put some warm water in this bowl and be back in a minute. You go ahead and lie on your stomach on the bed."

When he returned, she had followed his instructions. He set the bowl down and wet the washcloth, then ran it over the backs of her legs to dampen them. Then he shook the shaving cream and squirted a huge dollop into his hand.

Ashland sighed as he painted her legs with the cream. "That feels nice."

He smiled, reaching for the razor. "I'm going to shave now."

He removed the hair from the back of her legs slowly and carefully, checking to make sure he hadn't missed any. When he was done, he dampened the washcloth again and wiped the remaining traces of cream from her legs.

"Turn over," he instructed.

Ash turned onto her back. Damon stood over her, holding the eye mask. "I'd normally let you watch, but that's something that really brings out the beast in me, so it might be better if you wear the mask." He grinned. "Plus, I think you'll enjoy it."

"I will," she admitted. "I like not knowing exactly what's going to happen next." She took the mask from him and slipped it over her head.

"Raise your arms onto the pillow, over your head," he said.

She moved them up.

His fingers tickled her armpits as he rubbed the cream on. She closed her eyes, enjoying the sensation. She'd never been shaved before.

She liked it.

She started when his hand touched her belly. "I know they're short and fine," he explained, "but there are hairs on the belly, and it's already very sensitive, so I'd better take them off." His voice thickened. "Because I definitely want to wax your belly."

She shivered at the promise. "Yes, Damon."

He covered her tummy with the cool foam, then drew the razor gently across from side to side. Ash shivered again. God, the shaving part was damned erotic. She couldn't wait to get to the wax!

He did the front of her legs next, her pussy clenching as he parted them to take care of her inner thighs. After he wiped off the residue, he drew up her knees and pressed her legs apart.

Her pulse quickened. Oh, God. Was he going to shave her pussy, too?

He put a hand at her waist. "Lift your bottom, Ash."

She felt a pillow sliding under her, supporting her lower back and upper buttock area. Damon made a thoughtful sound; then she heard his footsteps leaving the room. When he returned, he had her raise up again and placed another pillow beneath her.

She felt the bed shift and knew he was climbing on, between her legs. "Perfect," he murmured.

She heard the squirt of foam and thought she was prepared, but she jumped when his hand glided over her bush.

Damon chuckled.

A line of cold about an inch and a half wide touched her abdomen. She shuddered. Damon drew the razor down slowly.

The prickling sensation as hair caught in the blades and parted before the razor sent chills up her spine. She shifted in response.

"You like that, huh?"

She nodded, not trusting her voice.

He carefully shaved her pubic mound, the experience driving her crazy. Then he pressed her clit to the side. Ash gasped, pussy spasming, as he removed the hair to one side, then the other.

He touched her legs. "A little further."

She spread them wide.

"Good."

He shaved the area just outside her labia, then placed his fingers at the outer edge of this newly shaved area and pulled her skin tight. "Don't move," he murmured.

She held her breath as he placed the razor at the inner border of her curls. As he drew the razor out toward his fingers, her pussy flooded with moisture.

He took three more passes to remove the hair, and Ash clutched at the pillow beneath her head, fighting the urge to wriggle.

When he started on the other side, she couldn't help it. Her pussy spasmed, once, twice.

"Ash," he admonished.

"I'm sorry. It feels so good," she moaned.

"Be patient, love." He pulled her skin tight again and finished that side quickly. He wiped the foamy traces off and ran his fingers over his handiwork.

"Oh, God," she moaned.

He laughed. "What's this?" he murmured. His finger ran up her slit. Ash arched, gasping. "Mmm. So juicy."

His weight shifted on the bed. She smelled her arousal as he brought his finger to her lips. "Open your mouth."

She obeyed, and he reached in, coating her tongue with her essence. She groaned, closing her mouth, sucking urgently.

"Uh-uh." A quick, sharp slap to her clit made her gasp. He pulled his finger out. "You do exactly as I tell you, Ash."

"Yes, Damon. I'm sorry."

"I was going to..." He slid his finger inside her pussy, then pulled it out before she could even react. "But now, you'll have to wait."

"No," she moaned.

"Oh, yes." He settled back between her legs.

She'd thought he was finished, but his hand slid between her cheeks. "Oh!" He pulled one cheek out, slathering cream onto it.

Ash trembled as he shaved one cheek, then the other, as close to her tight pucker as possible. Each stroke sent sultry spirals of arousal swirling from her ass to her pussy and back. "Oh, God, Damon," she whispered.

"Are you into ass play, baby?" he asked, sounding both surprised and pleased.

"God, yes," she groaned.

"I'll definitely remember that," he promised.

She heard the clatter of the razor being deposited on the tray. Then he pressed the washcloth between her cheeks, cleaning her, rubbing her anus briefly with one nubby, cloth-wrapped finger. Ash moaned, pleasure bursting in her groin.

Damon moved away. He lifted her legs, and the plastic rustled. "I'm drying things up," he explained.

A moment later, he said, "I'm testing the wax now, Ash. Making sure it won't burn you."

She pictured him holding the candle up, letting a drop fall on his inner wrist, making sure it was safe for her.

Seconds later, without warning, she felt warmth on the hollow at her throat, where her collarbones came together. The warmth moved in a narrow line down between her breasts, with occasional pauses.

"Mmm." She lifted her chin, arching slightly into the touch. Damon must be using the small paintbrush.

When the warmth reached her belly button, she heard a soft click and thought he might have put the brush down.

A cool droplet landed inside her belly button. "Oh!"

"Was it warm?" Damon asked.

She shook her head. Another drop, a little warmer. "Mmm."

"Better?"

"Yes."

Another drop, even warmer still. Ash sucked in a breath.

"Good enough?" he asked.

"A-a little closer," she suggested.

The next drop was just this side of hot. "Oh, God." She panted, her pulse racing. "Right there."

A stream of wax ran into the hollow. Ash gasped, clutching the corners of the pillow as her belly button filled.

"Too hot?"

"No," she rasped. "No, no. Just right."

The melted wax began to overflow, dribbling over the curve of her belly.

A brushful of wax painted in a circle along the outer edge of her areola came as a shock, so intent was she on the sensations around her middle.

"Oh!" Cold water dripped on her nipples; then ice touched the tips. "Oh, God."

Damon's warm mouth sucked the moisture off. "Damon," she moaned, tossing her head from side to side.

More ice. She breathed heavily as the cube circled her nipples, slid down between her breasts, tracing the previous line of wax, skipped over her belly button, continued down the other side, and pressed against her clit. "God, yes."

Then he slipped it into her pussy. "Oh, God."

"I don't want to see your pussy move," he warned.

"Oh, God, Damon. Please. I can't," she whimpered.

"You can."

Heat flowered on one nipple. "Oh, yes!" The sensation increased, edging almost into pain. "There!" she gasped.

Rivulets of wax trickled down. Between her breasts, down her sides. A new sensation every moment, unanticipated. She clenched her fists, straining to keep from squeezing her pussy tight, from arching her back or crying out.

She breathed in sharply as wax pooled in her armpits. She'd forgotten she even had her arms raised. She moaned, her breath coming in gasps.

"Ohmigod!" His hands, coated with wax, rubbed her pubis mons. She spread her legs wider.

Animal sounds escaped her as he continued to paint wax onto her with his hands, and then a fat dollop of liquid pleasure coated her clit.

She couldn't even cry out -- she couldn't form the thought. She arched.

"Not yet," Damon barked sternly.

"Damon, please," she begged.

"No."

She settled back to the bed, tears streaming from her eyes, but they were tears of excitement, tears of arousal. The longer he made her wait, the more intense she knew the orgasm would be.

His hands cupped her behind the knees and guided them back toward her, to either side of her chest. He grasped her hands and guided them into place. "Hold yourself just like that."

The wax in her armpit cracked as she moved, a surprisingly pleasant sensation.

Her buttocks parted and stayed parted. Something hard and cold held them in place. "My own little invention," he murmured. "I really like ass play."

She couldn't help it -- her pussy and ass clenched. Damon tsked. "Ash. At this rate, I'll never be able to give you what you want."

"Damon, please. It's so hard. It's been so long. I'm so *horny*." She knew she was babbling, but God, if he didn't let her come soon, she'd die.

A sliver of ice penetrated her anus. "Damon!"

"Squeeze it," he said. "But don't come."

She worked her ass.

She could hear Damon's breathing, louder now, becoming uneven. "Your ass is beautiful, Ash." Another sliver of ice, wider this time, slipped inside her. She squeezed eagerly. "Oh, yeah, baby. Your ass is blowing me big, wet kisses." He pressed another chip inside.

The bed shifted. His tongue swept over her flexing pucker. "Oh, God!" Her body trembled.

Warmth flowed between her cheeks. She gasped, moaned, drowning in sensation. The hot wax on her rim sent tendrils of bliss curling into her pussy, while the ice inside the canal relayed electric shivers to her clit. "Damon, *please.*"

"Not yet."

"Oh, God." She went limp against the bed.

Heat. Ice. Her fingers, toes. Ankles. Her clit again. She couldn't think anymore. There was only sensation. Curling and swirling, flitting and flickering within her like a candle flame. She was Damon's plaything. A toy. He could do anything he wanted with her.

Anything.

Remotely, she felt a warm, slick substance trickling between her buttocks and Damon rubbing at the wax on her clit, her pussy. Deep in subspace, she vaguely registered that he was slowly, gently, peeling it away.

"Ash." His voice in her ear startled her back to awareness.

"Yes?" she mumbled, her voice thick.

"Do you like the candles?"

"Mmm. Yes."

His fingers parted her labia. He tugged the eye mask from her head. "Watch, Ash."

He squirted some lube into his hands and picked up something from the bed beyond her line of sight.

She sucked in her breath.

He stroked a long, thick candle sensually, as though he were caressing his own cock. Ash felt a surge of excitement, her nipples tingling.

He pulled her legs back up to either side of her chest, and without being told, she held them in place.

"Good girl," he praised, and warmth washed over her.

He caught her eye, his features serious. "Don't scream, Ash. I don't think I can take that. Not yet."

She shook her head. "I won't, Damon," she croaked, voice hoarse with longing.

With the fingers of one hand he splayed her labia, and with the other sent the candle plunging into her, not slowing until it was buried inside her.

Her pussy stretched painfully. She gasped, then caught her bottom lip between her teeth as he drew it out and thrust it back in again.

Oh, God. Mmm. So thick.

It *hurt.* Just enough, not too much. Oh, yeah, he was good, just as she'd known he would be.

Her teeth tightened on her lip as she fought to keep from climaxing. The big wax dildo plunged in again and again. Faster, harder. "Damon, please," she gasped. "Please." She didn't know how much longer she could hang on.

She realized at that moment that he was naked. When had he taken his clothes off?

In one swift movement, he pulled back the dildo and buried his cock inside her. "Now, Ash!"

She arched, biting her lip to keep from screaming. Too hard -- a salty warmth trickled into her mouth, but she didn't care. His shaft filled her completely, hot and throbbing. She whimpered, bucking, pussy and ass clenching, bits of wax cracking and flaking off of her, adding their own unique array of sensations to her already overloaded body.

Pleasure slammed through her. She writhed, literally caught up in the maelstrom.

Damon roared. His hot seed poured into her, warming her, marking her. He held her hips immobile, groaning, shuddering, his cock buried deep inside her.

After their final shivers, Damon looked down at her. "I want you to stay so bad."

She opened her mouth to say yes, but he shook his head. "You can't. This was so good, but...right now I want nothing more than to tie you up and --" He shuddered. "I don't think I have that much control. Not yet. And if you're lying beside me in bed, I might just...well, I might not be able to resist trying. Let's take it slow, okay?"

She nodded. "I understand, Damon."

He ran the tip of a finger lightly over her bottom lip. "You're bruised."

"It was hard not to scream."

He bent his lips to hers and sucked the injured portion gently. Her nipples hardened instantly.

He drew back. "I hope I can let you scream. Soon." His eyes widened as he scanned her. "Umm…"

She raised her eyebrows. "What?"

"The rest of the wax."

"Oh. What about it?"

"I should remove it for you, but I think…" He drew in a shaky breath. "I don't think I can do it without wanting more."

"It's all right." Lord knew she didn't want to do anything to rush this process. She was beginning to honestly believe they might be able to build a relationship, despite his issues. "I can take care of it at home."

"I'm sorry."

"Don't apologize…Master." It wouldn't hurt to reinforce how strongly committed she was to him. "I don't mind at all."

His eyes went dark as she called him Master, and his lips curved in a slow, sensual smile. "Come back tomorrow, my sweet Ash. Ten in the morning. The rising sun floods this room, and I want to play with you in the daylight."

"Yes, Damon."

He groaned and rolled off of her. "You'd better go." He walked over to a closet and pulled out a spare sheet. "You can cover up with this." He grinned wickedly. "As a matter of fact, come back tomorrow dressed in this and nothing else.

She shivered. "Yes, Damon."

He wrapped the sheet around her shoulders, pulled her in for a kiss, then gave her a little push. "Go on. I'll see you in the morning."

"Yes, Master."

She let herself out and hurried back to her townhome.

Damon felt better than he had in a long time.

As he cleaned up, he reviewed the experience in his mind.

He'd remained in control, but it had been hard, toward the end. And every time Ash whimpered or moaned, he'd felt the ghostly images from Iraq trying to edge into his head. He'd been able to push them back, but the wax play they'd indulged in tonight had been fairly passive for him -- no real testing of her limits, no seriously physical aggression involved on his part. He wasn't sure he'd be so successful when they tried moving on to something more obviously painful.

Still, it was a promising start, and he couldn't wait for tomorrow.

He'd definitely sleep well tonight.

Chapter Thirteen: Pushing the Limit

Ashland peeked between her curtains and surveyed the townhomes in their cul-de-sac. At ten o'clock on a Sunday morning, it was pretty quiet. Those who went to the early church services were still there, and those who usually attended the latter ones wouldn't be heading out for another hour or so. The coast was clear.

She slipped outside, wrapped only in the sheet Damon had given her the night before. She turned her key in the lock quickly, heard the deadbolt slide shut, then dashed across the landing and rang Damon's doorbell.

He opened the door immediately. His gaze traveled down her body, a slow smile spreading across his face. "Good morning."

She knew she was grinning back at him like an idiot. "Hi."

He tucked an arm around her waist and drew her inside, kicking the door shut. "I missed you."

"I missed you, too."

Damon grasped the edges of the sheet where she held them together. She let go, and he pushed the sheet from her shoulders so that it pooled at her feet.

"Beautiful," he breathed.

Ash's cheeks grew hot, and it wasn't embarrassment. Just feeling his gaze on her body coaxed the flush of desire into her face, her chest. She knelt before him, clasping her arms behind her and bowing her head in submission.

He squatted in front of her, tilted her head up, and studied her rosy cheeks, her blushing breasts. "You want this, Ash."

It wasn't a question, but she answered anyway. "Yes, Master."

"Follow me."

He turned, and she rose and followed behind him. He took her back to the bedroom they'd used the night before. She didn't think it was the room he normally slept in. Though there was no specific indicator that led her to think that, it just didn't feel lived in.

On the other side of the bed was a large window in which the blinds had been drawn up so that light from the rising sun flooded the room. Damon walked over to the window and turned. "There," he said, and pointed.

She obediently stood where he'd indicated.

He'd been a busy boy this morning. Above her hung a shower curtain rod suspended from lengths of chain at each end that connected to sturdy hooks set into the ceiling.

"Raise your arms," Damon instructed. She did, and he pulled a short folding ladder from behind the dresser and stepped onto it, positioning Ash's arms and adjusting the lengths of the chains until he was satisfied.

"Stay still." He put the ladder away and reached into a large box sitting in front of the dresser, pulling out two lengths of marine rope. Ash cooperated eagerly as he bound each wrist to the shower rod device, about six inches in from their respective ends of the bar.

He reached into the box again, withdrawing a spreader bar with shackles attached.

Ash's pussy flooded with warmth. Damon knelt in front of her, guiding her legs into the position he desired, fastening her ankles into the shackles. When he was finished, he leaned in, resting his forehead against her tummy and taking a deep breath. "Mmm. You're ready for me, baby."

"Yes," she breathed.

He stood, letting his fingers glide from back to front between her wet lips, stopping to rub her clit. "So smooth," he murmured, running his hands over the skin usually covered in dark, curly hair. Direct, skin-to-skin contact there was so strange. She shivered, a bolt of desire piercing her clit. "You like that?"

She nodded, not trusting her voice.

"I'll want you smooth and clean sometimes, but sometimes I'll want you covered in curls so I can wrap them around my fingers." He pinched her clit, making her yelp. He grinned. "Give them a tug."

She panted at the thought. Damon's gaze drifted to her breasts. "Oops. Got sidetracked. That won't do." He reached into his box of tricks again, coming out with another length of chain. As he stepped up to her, he assured her, "I've double-checked every inch of this chain. I sanded every imperfection I thought might snag you, and wrapped it around myself several times to check for comfort. It's as safe as I can make it."

She nodded. "I trust you, Damon."

He breathed in sharply, let it out slowly. "I know you do, baby."

He began wrapping the links around her. "I've wanted to do this ever since that night with your belt."

Cold, the metal pressed into her. He framed her nipples perfectly within two large links, then wrapped the ends around her back, guiding them around and forward again under her armpits. Crossing them above her breasts, he draped them over her shoulders, crossed them again in the back, and wrapped them back around front beneath her breasts. He continued until both of her generous orbs protruded prominently from between two top and bottom layers, with the original framing links drawn taut against her areoles, her rock-hard nipples tingling.

"Because this is a new relationship for us, I want to let you know what safety measures I've taken every step of the way." He spoke softly in her ear as he secured the chain. "I'm fastening this with a quick-release hook." He stepped around to face her and studied his handiwork. "Oh, yes. I like that."

Ash nodded mutely in agreement, weak-kneed with anticipation. She drank in the sight of him. Dressed in tight black jeans and a pair of black tennis shoes, he was shirtless, his tanned, toned body just about perfect. She'd never realized how muscular he was, his biceps flexing as he reached down yet again into the wonderful toy box.

He pulled out a cloth-wrapped bundle and set it on the dresser, unfolding the fabric and setting out a variety of items -- two stainless-steel chopsticks, some of the flexible metal hair clips that just had to be bent to fasten and unfasten, a tube of toothpaste, a vegetable scrubbing mitt, bottles with labels she couldn't see well enough to read from her current position, and more.

Mmmm. He was going to drive her crazy.

Her pussy wept, the musky scent of her growing stronger. Damon picked up an item and advanced toward her.

Eyes on her face, he sucked a taut, swollen nipple into his mouth.

"Oh, God!" The soft warmth of his mouth felt so good in contrast with the hard, cold metal biting into her. She stared into his eyes, moaning.

His hand slipped between her legs, harvesting her juices. He smeared them on her breasts, reaching down twice for more, then reached down again and --

"Oh!" Her clit stung, pinched by the hair clip. "Oh, yes!"

Damon took his time cleaning her breasts of her juices, wet tongue darting between the smooth metal links, teasing her nipples, biting at her exposed flesh lightly with his teeth, bringing forth an involuntary chorus of sighs and gasps. Her clit pulsed, fingers of pain and pleasure gliding back and forth between the tortured nub and her pussy.

Her breasts and nipples ached, the chain pressing into them, the chill of cold metal vying with the heated desire rising within her. She shuddered.

Damon reached down, releasing the improvised clit clamp, and Ash cried out.

He placed a finger to her lips. "Shhh," he reminded her, a warning look in his eyes.

"Yes, Damon," she whispered.

He grabbed the tube of toothpaste from the dresser and squeezed a dab onto his finger.

Watching her expression, he smeared the minty mixture onto her clit. "Mmm. Your little clit's not so little anymore, baby. It's plump and ripe." Rubbing, rubbing, he worked the nub, then pulled his hand away.

Ash gasped. A tingling sensation built between her legs. She breathed hard, wanting him to touch her again, to give the nub a good hard pinch, a twist, *anything.*

The sensation intensified. Stinging. Oh, God. *Burning.* She wanted to scream, but didn't dare. God. She couldn't take it, and yet she didn't want it to stop. It hurt so *good*, piercing forks of pleasure shooting through her clitoris. And her breasts, bound and throbbing, sent their own delicious signals as well. She moaned, letting her head fall back, trying to wiggle but unable to do anything because she was bound.

"Damon, please." She sobbed, trying to thrust her pelvis at him. "Please!"

He knelt, grinning wickedly. Bringing his mouth close to the swollen nugget, he parted his lips and breathed out, warm, moist air that caressed her, then pursed his lips and leaned away a little, blowing cold across the sensitive peak.

"Oh, God, Master! Please, please…" Her voice trailed away to a whimper.

"What is it, Ash?" he asked softly.

"Touch me. Please," she begged. "Please, touch my pussy. I'm so horny. Please."

He stood and stared into her eyes, his finger finding and teasing the nub gently. "Come for me, Ash," he commanded. "Come quick and hard."

His free hand gripped her waist, holding her tight while his finger circled, pressing harder, faster. Ash started to arch again, but the hand at her waist lifted to grasp her braid and hold her head in place. "No. Look at me."

His fingers pinched, and a tiny squeal escaped before she managed to clamp her lips down. She gazed into his eyes, knowing her own were drunk with pleasure.

She shivered uncontrollably as wave after wave of bliss washed over her.

"That's it," Damon whispered. "Oh, Ash. I wish you could see the way you look when you come. So sexy. Your eyes so dark and full of passion. Flushed with desire."

His fingers slid into her pussy.

"Yes!" She spasmed, every muscle in her body seeming to contract at the same time, trying to press in against him, feel him inside her as the final, mind-numbing climax rushed through her. "Oh, God, Damon. Oh, God." Her breasts swelled even more, flushed with her arousal.

He caught her bottom lip between his teeth, sucking on the portion she'd bruised the night before as he drew his fingers out, painting her shaved mons with her sticky juices. Her clit still burned, but the sensation was fading, the toothpaste rubbed away by his fingers and diluted by the evidence of her arousal.

She moaned as her orgasm passed. Her body wanted to collapse, but with the spreader bar between her legs and her wrists tied to the suspension above, that was impossible.

Her knees trembled as Damon moved away, which he noticed. "Are you all right? Do we need to take a break?"

"No." She took a deep breath and let it out. "No, please. I'm fine," she whispered throatily.

"Good girl."

She thrilled at his praise.

He disappeared behind her. She felt a slight tightening of the links around her chest, then experienced a rush of both pain and pleasure as the ovals released her skin reluctantly, leaving behind pale oval indentations surrounding engorged, reddened areas of her flesh.

Damon peeled the chain away and surveyed his handiwork. "Mmm. Nice." He went to the dresser and picked up a camera she hadn't noticed before. "Pictures for our scrapbook," he remarked, snapping a series of photos from different angles as he circled her. "We *will* keep a scrapbook and look through it together often, discussing how you look, what we might do differently, what we'll try next." He was in front of her again, his gold-brown eyes gazing into hers. "Would you like that, baby?"

"Yes," she whispered. "Oh, yes, Damon."

He set the camera down and grabbed a collar, as well as one of several gloves waiting on the dresser. It had a rough inner surface, a glove used for washing vegetables. Giving her a sultry glance, he strolled around behind her again.

She sucked in her breath as he placed the collar around her neck. "You're mine, now, Ash." He fastened it and checked the fit. "Isn't that right?" he whispered in her ear.

She started to nod, but the collar wouldn't permit it, so she answered breathlessly. "Yes, Damon. I'm yours. I belong to you."

The collar had two extremely long leather leashes fastened to its ring. Damon slipped these between her legs and tugged them into the crevice between her cheeks. The leather rubbed against her clit, and she moaned. "Good sub," Damon murmured. "Hot, sexy sub." Her pussy wept, her juices running down the insides of her legs. "Mmmm." Damon's breath tickled her ear. "Your smell fills the room. This is *our* room, baby." His fingers glided along her crack, tucking the leather against her. "The things I'm going to do to you in here…"

"Damon. Oh, my God." She groaned.

"Shh." He pulled the loose ends of leather around her waist and back to the front, crossed them, then reached up and wrapped them around the bar above her, sliding them out toward her bound wrists.

Oh! Ash gasped in delight as the leather strips tightened, parting her cheeks, tugging them aside.

Damon peeked over her shoulder. "That should do it." He tied the ends in place on the bar.

He disappeared behind her again.

A few seconds passed, and then his gloved hand touched her. Abrasive, its scratchy substance rubbed the exposed insides of her cheeks, first one, then the other, not quite touching her puckered anus. She moaned, wanting to squirm, knowing it was futile.

The insides of her cheeks first itched, then burned. Her anus throbbed. She held her breath, waiting.

Finally, he rubbed a rough-surfaced, gloved finger across the tight pucker. "Yes, Damon, yes."

Again and again, he ran his finger up and down her crack, scritching, scratching. Ash moaned as heat flooded her thighs, her groin, her pussy. "Please, Master," she begged. "Please. Put it inside me."

"Are you sure?" His voice sounded strained. Her heart leapt at this evidence of his desire.

"Yes, Sir. Please, Master. Please." Her voice trembled with need.

She heard him draw a sharp breath. Her pussy clenched as he thrust a gloved finger deep inside it, wetting the gloved digit, slicking it with her juices.

He stood and wrapped one arm around her waist.

No warning. Rough nubs penetrating her ass. Her taut pucker clenched violently.

"Damn!" He burrowed deeper, her ass itching, stinging, sending sparks of heat and desire showering through her.

Oh, so nice. She felt the tension of the previous few weeks draining away. The anxiety over Damon, the day-to-day struggles to maintain a profitable business, all melted into nothingness. Pain was her release, and her pleasure. Her safety valve.

Her ass tightened around his wonderful toy.

"God, Ash." He groaned. "I never thought..." He probed deeply, and her ass clenched again and again. "I didn't know how much you could take."

"Fuck me," she rasped. "Master, please. Fill me with your cock. Let my ass drink your seed."

"Ash." Her name was a sigh.

His finger worked. Rougher now, faster, as she heard the pop of a snap, a zipper parting, the rustle of his tight jeans as he peeled himself out of them.

Abruptly, the sweet torture disappeared.

"No," she moaned.

Wordlessly, Damon grabbed the short ladder and set it out, stepping up to release the chains above her and lower the bar. "Bend over," he ordered.

Stiff, she let him guide her into a curve over the back of the stepladder, a movement that drew the leather straps even tauter where they gripped her cheeks, exposing her puckered anus even more.

"Wait." He snatched a pillow from the bed and put it over the ladder back, padding it for her. "There."

He grabbed a couple of oblong metal spring clips and grasped the chains hanging from either end of the rod. Tugging them down, he fastened each end to a corresponding leg on the ladder, just below a step so that there was a "stop" that kept them from sliding further up the leg. The arrangement held her in place, exposing her ass completely.

"Yes," Ash sobbed. "Yes, Damon. This is what I want."

Cool oil poured over her cheeks, gliding down her crack, pooling on the carpet beneath her. "Yes," she whispered. "Yes."

His finger plunged into her, slick and warm, flesh to flesh, the glove gone. "Yes!"

He pushed another in, stretching her, his breathing heavy behind her, his voice thick as he said, "You have such a big, beautiful ass, baby. So damn fuckable." Her muscles constricted around the two questing fingers. "God, yes, Ash." He moaned. "Take me, baby." He twisted his fingers slowly, spreading them apart a little, reaming the tight opening, preparing her.

"Another," she gasped.

His fingers froze. The very air in the room seemed to wait in anticipation.

Her ass stretched as he growled, forcing a third finger deep inside her.

Ash screamed. "Yes! Yes." She whimpered, trying to rock back. "Yes, Master."

His free arm slipped under her, grasping the opposing rail of the ladder back, and he thrust his fingers in, out, in, out.

Ash screamed again, the pain a sweet release.

Damon faltered.

She felt him hesitating, drawing back.

"No, Damon, no," she cried out. "Please don't stop. Please," she begged. "Please fuck me. Please!"

"Ash, I --"

"I want it, Damon!" She tightened her anal muscles on his fingers deliberately, over and over, knowing how it turned him on. "I need it. It's *my* pain, Damon. Mine. Not yours. Not *theirs.* I need this. I have to have it. Please." Her voice trailed away to a whisper. "This isn't war, Damon. It's love. Our love."

He shuddered, bending over, pressing his face against her back. "The screams," he muttered desperately.

"Screams of excitement, Damon," she insisted. "Joy." His fingers were moving ever so slightly, up and down inside her. Good. His body knew what he wanted, even if his mind fought it. "Screams don't only come from fear and loss. They express pleasure and fulfillment.

"Please, Damon." She closed her eyes and prayed as she spoke, prayed that he would listen. "I love you. All of you. Don't hide any longer. Not from me."

His body shook. He edged away from her, his fingers retracting. *No. No!*

She'd lost him.

The sudden grief turned into shock as his cock slammed against her puckered ass. She gasped, fingers clutching at the bar. His hands gripped her waist. *Yes. Oh, please, yes. Don't let him stop.* His cockhead stretched her, her tight rim pulsing as his delicious cock eased past.

He pulled back and penetrated her again, faster this time, driving himself deep inside her.

"Oh, God, yes. Yes, Damon."

He slid out, then forced himself in again, fast, his balls slapping against her exposed pussy as he finally buried himself completely.

Ash groaned. Her ass throbbed and ached, tingled, the sensations tugging at the hot core of need within her.

He thrust again. Harder. Faster.

She whimpered, fingers squeezing on the bar.

His hands tightened at her waist. He pounded into her.

Yes! She shuddered, spears of pleasure shooting between her legs, piercing her nipples. She cried out, unable to keep from doing so, and this time Damon answered her by quickening his pace, thrusting in and out, fucking her, fucking her hard.

He grabbed her braid, tugging her head up and back.

"Yes, yes!" Ash arched as much as she could, trying to rock back to meet him. "Yes."

She was his. Every particle of her being melted in the knowledge that she belonged to him, that he cared enough about her to fight his demons and be what she needed him to be.

She felt herself drifting into that state of release, where all the pressures of the world faded away. There was nothing but this moment. The bliss she was experiencing, *and* the pain, a perfect medley that carried her into subspace, floating on a river of sensation as he penetrated her again and again.

She drifted in subspace, waiting. Waiting breathlessly for…

His pelvis slammed against her, his balls slapping her pussy.

"Damon!"

His hands held tight to her braid, keeping her arched, holding her still as his cock swelled. She could feel the heat of his seed, filling her, soothing her.

"God!" Ash shivered uncontrollably as wave after wave of delightful fulfillment washed over her. Her pussy wept. Her tight ass throbbed, closing hungrily on Damon's pulsing cock.

So good. No word could do justice to what she was feeling right then, so she quit trying to find one. She just rode the waves, drowning in pleasure, screaming with joy.

Damon held on to Ash, her braid a lifeline, keeping him afloat in a storm of sensation and emotion. Images crashed over him, of the dead and dying, the injured and maimed, their screams of terror echoing in his mind, a gray veneer over the sound of her pleasure.

But faintly, beneath it all, resonated his sweet Ash.

Generous and giving. Honest and open.

So alive and vibrant. So ready to *feel* everything, to revel in her differences.

And in *his*.

A flash of her face in the mirror at her apartment, cheeks flushed, eyes glazed and unfocused as he played with her pussy.

Her watching him, hot and horny, as he fucked her with a candle.

Sly glances from beneath her lashes at him across the table, as she played with her nipples during that first date, their night at the restaurant.

And her screams, her moans, her sighs.

A beautiful symphony of surrender and delight.

Tension drained from him as he slammed into her one last time, his cock buried deep inside her hot little hole as the last of his semen gushed, pulsing into her as her tight pucker squeezed and suckled.

Yes. This was it. This was him. What he wanted, what he needed. The only way to stay sane.

She was screaming for him, arched and sweating, a smile plastered across her beautiful face.

Ash wanted it. Wanted it *all.*

He closed his eyes and gave her everything, shivering as the new memories they were making washed away the old.

Chapter Fourteen: A Beast Awakened

Ash checked her watch for the umpteenth time. It was a Saturday, but she'd had to go in to the lab to fill in for a sick employee, and now an accident on the interstate was making her late for her date with Damon. She caught her lower lip between her teeth in frustration. The week before, when he had fucked her ass so deliciously, she had known that there was no one else for her. It was Damon or no one.

He'd felt guilty afterward because he *had* lost control, as far as he was concerned. She'd been afraid he was going to go all cold on her again, but he hadn't. He *had* eventually sent her home, because he said there was no way he could keep his hands off her and if he did everything to her that he *wanted* to do that day, she wouldn't be able to walk for a week.

Ash shivered at the memory. Knowing he wanted her so much made all the confusion and disappointment leading up to their latest encounter worth it.

He'd been over for dinner every night this week, but they hadn't been intimate. She smiled at the memory of their quiet conversations. He'd said he wanted to get to know her mind as well as her body. They'd talked for hours, and she loved him all the more now that she knew him even better.

It had been a hell of a week at work. As a matter of fact, her conversations with Damon had been interrupted twice by calls from her night staff. She'd had to leave, and to her relief, he'd been fine with that. She'd have to wait and see how he reacted when it happened in the middle of a sexual encounter, but she had a feeling everything was going to be fine on that front, as well. He did not seem intimidated by her public position. He knew that, in every way that mattered, she belonged to no one but *him*.

He'd also said the wait would do them some good. She didn't know about *that*. What it *had* done was make her incredibly horny and created a lot of sleepless nights spent tossing and turning, unable to relieve her sexual tension because Damon had warned her never to touch herself without his permission.

Finally, the traffic before her started moving. Ash tapped her steering wheel impatiently as she edged forward, slowly at first, then faster as the highway opened up before her.

Damon was waiting for her when she stepped out of the car.

"You're late," he admonished.

"I know." She hung her head. "There was a wreck on four-oh-one. I'm sorry."

"You can't control the traffic," he admitted, "But next time, call me."

"Yes, Damon."

He led the way to his home, opened the door, and ushered her inside.

Ash shed her clothes immediately, as he had instructed her to do when they'd spoken the night before.

"Good girl," he said, eyeing her hungrily.

She swallowed, her breasts tingling.

"Four," he said.

Ash dropped to her knees, spreading her legs wide, placing her hands behind her head, fingers interlaced, face forward, assuming that particular presentation position.

"Good girl." Damon squatted and reached between her legs, dipping his fingers up into her pussy, then pulled them out and licked her essence from them. "Mmm." He smiled. "You're very wet, cinnamon." He'd chosen "cinnamon" as her sub name, explaining that it reminded him of how she'd tasted the very first time they kissed, and that it was hot and spicy, like her. She'd thrilled at the praise.

"Yes, Master," she agreed. "I get very wet when I'm thinking of you."

"And how often is that?" he asked, grinning.

"Always," she purred throatily.

He laughed. "Oh, baby. You make me very happy."

He took off his shirt and tossed it over the back of the couch. "Undress me," he commanded.

Ash slipped his shoes from his feet and placed them to the side. She rolled his socks down and slipped them off, folded them, and laid them neatly on top of his shoes. She unfastened his jeans and shimmied them down past his hips to the ankles, where he stepped out of them. Then she removed his briefs, freeing his feverish, ripe cock.

"May I suck you, Master?"

He frowned down at her. "No, you may not." Then he smiled. "I have a surprise for you."

He held out his hand and led her down the hall to their room.

"Oh, Sir!" She clapped her hands together in delight. Their play room now held a gorgeous four-poster bed in a lustrous dark wood. He'd fastened rings to each post, to which lengths of ropes were now tied, and covered it in a sumptuous white lace ensemble. She looked at him. "It's beautiful, but...white lace?" It seemed an odd choice.

He flashed his wicked grin. "Oh, I thought the contrast with *this* would be very interesting." He turned and went to the closet, pulled something out, and came back, draping it over the bed.

It was a black suede outfit with purple stitching, looking deliciously naughty against the sweet innocence of the bedding.

"Put it on."

Ash obeyed immediately. She tugged on the black mesh stockings with their cut-out crotch. She stepped into the corsetlike costume, shimmying to get it over her hips. Damon moved behind her and, once she had it all the way up, tugged on the laces, pulling them tight, tighter, until her waist was cinched and her breasts bulged from the top.

"Mmm. Nice." He picked up his camera. "Sit on the bed."

She sat on the edge.

"Scoot back," he said. "Sit Indian style. I want to get a picture of that hot, wet pussy."

Warmth flooded her abdomen. She slid back and tugged her legs up, crossing them as he wanted.

"Lean back on your arms."

She complied, her pulse racing as he snapped a quick succession of pictures from different angles.

He grinned. "Now, lay on your side, with the top leg cocked." He took more pictures, immortalizing her body on film as her pussy became wetter and wetter.

"Touch yourself," he instructed, his voice thick.

Pulse racing, Ash reached down and toyed with her clit. Damon's breathing quickened. She let her fingers slide down. Parting her pussy lips with the second and fourth fingers of one hand, she glided the long middle finger in and out of her pussy, nipples tightening at the faint, wet sounds she made.

"Mmmm." She found her sweet spot and started fucking herself in earnest. Damon watched, snapping an occasional picture, his eyes dark with desire as her pace increased.

"Stop!" He uttered the command just before she came. Ash moaned, trembling, pulling her finger out reluctantly.

Damon set the camera aside and approached her. "Lay back."

She scooted to the middle of the bed and lay down, spread-eagled. Damon's eyes were hot with promise as he tied her wrists to the posts at the head of the bed, and her ankles to the foot posts.

He walked over to the desk and picked up a crop. Ash's eyes widened as she took in the slender rod, with a six-inch flogging braid attached to the tip.

She trembled as he ran the braid over the swell of her breasts, then down between them to the peak of her exposed clit.

She gasped at the touch of the cool length of the crop gliding across her clit.

He flicked the braid.

"Oh!" She squirmed, her clit stinging in that oh-so-right way.

He smiled wickedly and flicked the crop again.

"Oh, God."

The next stroke kissed her pussy. She writhed, hoping he would press the flogger inside.

He laughed, as though having read her mind. "Not yet, my sweet cinnamon."

He flicked her again and again, the braid getting wet with her juices, landing cool and damp on her inner thighs, her shaved mons.

"Yes, Master, yes!" She wriggled and writhed, trying to position herself so that the flogger tip would slip inside her, but Damon watched, tormenting her, keeping it just out of reach.

He reached out and worked his hand inside the top of her corset, tugging her breasts from their tight confines.

The wet flogger stung her nipples. "God, yes," she sobbed. "Yes, Damon."

His hand smacked her clit. "Master or Sir, cinnamon."

"Yes, Sir. Master!"

"I was going to reward you, but now…" Ash moaned as he set aside the flogger. He picked up a long, nubby vibrator. Grinning, he pressed it into her slick pussy.

"Oh, God, Master."

He turned it on. Ash moaned again.

"I'm going to let you lie there and think about your mistake for a while, cinnamon."

She groaned, her muscles clenching.

The vibrator slid out.

"Uh-oh. We'll have to fix that." Damon grabbed a scarf from the dresser and folded it into a three-inch-wide strip. Pushing the dildo deep inside her, he made her raise her hips so he could fasten the ends of the strip to the back and front of her costume with clamps. "That should do it."

"Sir, please…" Ash begged.

"You know you have to be disciplined."

She lowered her gaze. "Yes, Sir."

"Don't allow yourself to come."

"No, Sir."

He left the room without another word, leaving the door open so that he could check on her frequently and hear her if she just couldn't take any more and used her safe word.

Ash lay trembling, weak with need. The vibrator pulsed, bathing her pussy and ass in delicious, buzzing sensation. She moaned, shifting, fighting the instinct to clench her muscles tight around it.

She focused her mind on the sensations. The muted vibration, the ball of warmth slowly gathering in her abdomen.

Her nipples flushed dark, plumping. The ball of warmth grew, spreading down between her legs, up into her torso. She tossed her head.

Her body ached for fulfillment. Ash closed her eyes, feeling only the pulsing inside her, straining to keep herself from responding, from disappointing her Master.

She lost track of time. Felt tension drain from her, replaced by the soothing, constant ache of desire.

The heat in her middle spread, plumping her breasts, warming her arms, her fingers and toes.

She was nothing, nothing but a hot, wet pussy, aching to be filled, desperate for release, hungry for her Master.

"Come now," his sweet voice whispered in her ear.

She arched. His hand pressed the dildo deep inside her, holding it in place while he flicked her clit.

Ash screamed, her release a rush of flickering heat, racing in her veins, that hot core within her bursting into a thousand pleasant sensations that fluttered in her tummy, tickled her thighs, danced atop her breasts.

Aching and weak, she collapsed against the bed when it passed. She felt a tug as Damon released the clamp on the front of her outfit and tugged the vibrator from inside her.

She felt the bed shift as he climbed up onto it, and opened her eyelids.

His golden irises looked deep into her darker bronze. "I think you've learned your lesson."

"Yes, Master," she whispered.

He smiled. Turned and untied first one ankle, then the other.

He raised her legs, pushing her knees back toward either side of her chest and holding them there.

"I'm going to fuck you now, cinnamon. Hard and fast."

"Yes, Sir. Please, Sir," she rasped. "Please, please, fuck me."

He stroked into her, her pussy so wet that he glided in smoothly. "Mmm. You feel so nice," he murmured. "All hot and wet, surrounding me completely."

He buried his length, resting there, watching her face as she became more and more anxious, wanting to flex her pussy but knowing he would discipline her again if she did.

"Master," she whispered when she wasn't sure she could take any more.

He drew back so fast, she almost thought his cock would pop out, but then he was inside her again. In and out, fast and furious, her legs spread back and pressed open wide so he could pound deep inside her, fill her completely, stroke her and stroke her, until --

"Master!"

He froze, grinning down at her as her pussy clutched his cock, over and over again. As she moaned and writhed and uttered little animal sounds, riding the crest of another incredible orgasm.

And just as it began to fade...

His eyes went dark. He stiffened, his back arching slightly. His hands tightened on her thighs, his eyes staring into hers as his warmth bathed her, filled her, sent her shuddering into another release, her mouth open in a wordless cry, fingers wrapped tight around the ropes that bound her.

When it was over, he gently untied her wrists and lay down beside her, cradling her head on his chest. "God, Ash. You're so remarkable."

She smiled sleepily. In this bedroom, when he called her Ash, she was released from the need to address him as Master or Sir and could enjoy the pleasure saying his name gave her. "Only for you, Damon."

He pinched her nipple playfully. "Damn right."

He sighed contentedly. "I always wanted to train a woman to come on command, but I think you're already there." He shivered, looking down at her, his eyes filled with wonder. "When I touched you, whispered in your ear, watched you shudder and felt your body clenching, you looked so beautiful. I'm so glad you want what I have to give."

Ash snuggled close. "I love you, Damon."

"I love you, too, Ash."

His hand stroked her forehead, her cheek. He reached over to the bedside table and pressed a button on the remote that controlled the overhead lights and fan, and the room plunged into darkness.

Ash fell asleep to the steady rhythm of his heart and his tender caress.

Chapter Fifteen: Gifts for the Gifted

Months later, Damon sat in a restaurant booth, smiling down at the lovely woman by his side. Over the last few months, she'd helped him conquer the lingering traces of emotional trauma from Iraq. He was happier than he'd ever been, had received a commendation from his sergeant, and the phantoms had all but disappeared.

It was all because of her.

Ash looked gorgeous in her tight knit tee with its insubstantial, built-in bra that did nothing to hide the way her nipples were plumping as he worked her pussy with his fingers -- beneath her skirt, under the table.

The waitress came and took their order. Ash flushed and stammered a bit, but got her order out. Usually he ordered for her, but he'd wanted to watch her speak while he was finger-fucking her, knowing the woman taking her request did not have any idea what was going on.

As they finished ordering and the woman walked away, she sighed, leaning into him, spreading her legs a little wider.

He grinned, tugging his fingers free, ignoring her whispered protest.

He slid her teaspoon from the table.

Slipped it between her legs.

"Keep it there," he ordered, and her eyes went dark with desire, making his balls ache.

He made her eat with one hand, his cock growing hard and straining against his slacks as he thought of her other fingers, busy diving and dipping into her pussy, gliding the spoon in and out beneath the table.

In the car when they left, she reclined sideways in the seat and spread her legs.

His eyes drank their fill on the ride home, his hand wandering at will. At a stoplight, the driver in a truck next to them glanced into the Jeep, catching Damon in the act of running his fingers along her seeping slit. The man grinned and gave him a high-five sign. Damon grinned back.

She was sopping wet by the time they pulled into the townhomes' parking circle. The sun had set, and there was no one around.

"Ash," he murmured.

"Hmm?"

He held out a hand, helping her sit up, and leaned in close to her ear. "Fuck my gear shift, like you promised."

There and gone almost before he could see it, a tremor shook her whole body.

"Yes," she whispered.

"Wait." He reached into the glove box, removing a package of antibacterial wipes.

He cleaned the shifter, then grinned at her.

Ash hiked up her skirt, straddling the gear shift.

Damon watched in the lamplight as she worked her pussy over the thick knob. She'd told him she'd always wanted to have a lover who drove a stick shift, just so she could fuck the shifter while he watched. It was one of the many fantasies they'd shared with each other.

"Oh, God," she moaned.

He reached beneath her skirt, found her hot little anus, and pressed his finger inside.

She bucked, ripe and ready from the constant fondling during dinner. Arching, she came, cheeks and chest blushing dark, biting her lip to keep from crying out where the neighbors might hear her.

She was so vocal he'd had to line the inside of their playroom with acoustic tile, to keep their lovemaking from disturbing the neighbors.

"Mmm, Ash," he murmured as she whimpered softly, body spasming while her pussy clutched the gear shift and her anus sucked at his finger. "You are such a sexy, perfect sub."

He wrapped an arm around her, felt her sag as the orgasm passed, and lifted her from the shifter. "Nice. Now I'll think of you every time I drive." As if he didn't already. "And smell you on my hand."

She shivered.

He smiled to himself and stepped out, then went around and opened the door for her.

Inside his townhome, he stripped her in the living room and knelt before her, sucking her clit until she clutched his shoulders, shuddering as she came for the second time that night.

He reached beneath the sofa, pulling out a large box with a smaller one sitting atop it. "Ash."

She looked down. When their eyes met, he sensed the tension of the day starting to drain from her. Glimmers of the look he loved to give her -- of contentment, of perfect bliss -- appeared in her eyes, in the curving corners of her mouth.

"Yes, Master?" She grinned. It was okay to call him by his name when he used hers, but when she was feeling especially submissive -- or horny -- she threw in a Master or three at times like these, which could really get him going.

His sweet sub knew what he liked.

What he *loved.*

So did he.

He raised the small box in his hand and opened the lid. "Will you marry me, Ashland Finn?"

Her eyes filled with tears, wonder and joy radiating from her. "Damon, really?"

"Yes." He kissed her ample tummy, his favorite pillow. Over the last few months, he'd slept with his head resting on her well-padded belly more times than he could count. Why he'd ever thought he preferred his women slim, he'd never know. "I don't ever want to sleep separate from you again. I want to take you with me when my tour of duty ends here. Wherever I go, I want you by my side. You're a part of me, Ash. You bring out the best in me." And Damon Wayland's best was a Dominant who now was content in his job, well-liked by his coworkers, and totally in love with the woman he was kneeling before.

"I hardly know what to say, Master," she breathed, eyes bright with mischief.

So he told her, as she'd known he would.

"Say yes."

Epilogue

Damon walked into the Trianon Bar on the thirteenth floor of the Ritz Carlton in Chicago with his new bride on his arm.

Ash glowed in a pale yellow dress that accentuated her golden tan. An intricate braid, which she'd learned how to do especially for the wedding and had taken a liking to, rested against her back, mahogany dark with auburn highlights gleaming. They'd gotten married the evening before in Texas, then flew into Chicago and spent their first night together as husband and wife in the honeymoon suite.

He grinned. And a wild night it had been. He might never be able to see a Jacuzzi tub again without getting a raging hard-on.

On his wife's left hand were her engagement ring and wedding band, and around her neck was a circlet of leather with diamonds set between silver studs -- the item from the other box he'd given her on the night of his proposal.

To everyone else, it was just a choker.

For those in the know, it was an unmistakable sign of ownership.

He spotted Baldie at the bar. By his side was a slim African-American woman with striking brown eyes.

Damon guided Ash over. "Baldwin!"

"Hey, Damon!" His high school buddy shook his hand. "Glad you could make it, man!"

Damon nodded. "I'd like to introduce my wife, Ash. Ash, this is Baldwin Garrett."

"Your wife! When'd you get married?"

"Yesterday, actually. I took next week off -- we're going to make this trip into a honeymoon escape."

Ash shook Baldie's hand, saying, "I've heard a lot about you."

His old friend laughed. "Uh-oh." He turned to his companion, his blue eyes sparkling. "This is my girl, Kena Rutherford." She smiled and shook hands as well.

As the women turned away, Kena exclaiming over Ash's rings, Baldie raised his eyebrows and tilted his chin to indicate the band around Ash's neck.

Damon nodded.

"Congrats, man. You're living the dream."

Damon glanced at Kena. "I think we both are."

Baldwin's eyes went soft as his gaze rested on the attractive woman. "Yeah, we are, come to think of it."

"Damon! Baldwin!"

He glanced up to see Rich approaching, leading a very attractive couple. He stifled some surprise. Straight-laced

Rich in a ménage? He wouldn't have thought it. But it was obvious from their posture and the way their bodies brushed against each other as they walked that the three of them were physically intimate.

And Mike strode in just behind them, a muscular guy with piercing green eyes in tow. *Ah-ha.*

Well, the gang was all there, and it was shaping up to be a very interesting evening.

Not, of course, nearly as interesting as the nights he had planned for Ash…

~ * ~

Rachel Bo

Rachel Bo is an award-winning author currently published in several genres. On the weekends, she works as a Clinical Laboratory Scientist. During the week, Rachel writes and rides herd on her handsome husband, two wonderful daughters, a rabbit, a snake and several remarkably hardy goldfish.

Learn more about Rachel and her upcoming releases at http://webpages.charter.net/rachelbo/, or feel free to e-mail her at rachbo03@yahoo.com.

ANTHOLOGIES AVAILABLE In Print from Loose Id®

HARD CANDY
Angela Knight, Sheri Gilmore & Morgan Hawke

HOWL
Jet Mykles, Raine Weaver & Jeigh Lynn

RATED: X-MAS
Rachel Bo, Barbara Karmazin & Jet Mykles

ROMANCE AT THE EDGE: IN OTHER WORLDS
MaryJanice Davidson, Angela Knight & Camille Anthony

THE BITE BEORE CHRISTMAS
Laura Baumbach, Sedonia Guillone & Kit Tunstall

WILD WISHES
Stephanie Burke, Lena Matthews & Eve Vaughn

Publisher's Note: The print titles listed above were previously released in e-book format by Loose Id®.

Non-fiction from Loose Id®

PASSIONATE INK
ANGELA KNIGHT

OTHER TITLES AVAILABLE In Print from Loose Id®

COURTESAN
Louisa Trent

DANGEROUS CRAVINGS
Evangeline Anderson

DINAH'S DARK DESIRE
Mechele Armstrong

HEAVEN SENT: HELL & PURGATORY
Jet Mykles

HEAVEN SENT 2
Jet Mykles

STRENGTH IN NUMBERS
Rachel Bo

THE TIN STAR
J. L. Langley

THE BROKEN H
J. L. Langley

Publisher's Note: The print titles listed above were previously released in e-book format by Loose Id®.

Printed in the United States
207969BV00001B/64/P